CRITICAL ACCLAIM

"Dabydeen is a short story master ... narratives deal with love and friendship triangles, human relationships at the personal level, but also with the coming together of countries and continents: 'Asia, Africa, America — all one with the stars moving above.' They prove that Cyril Dabydeen is a writer of global concerns, permanently crossing boundaries."

— *Canadian Literature*

"His stories are seamless between past and present, fantasy and reality ... a significant post-colonial writer."

— *World Literature Today*

"Cyril Dabydeen ... is a consistent and eloquent witness of the man-on-the-way, the traveller, the pilgrim. He captures the spirit of the displaced, the dislocated, and the alien within the Canadian experience."

— *Canadian Ethnic Studies*

"There is a kaleidoscopic quality to these short stories, a shifting and colliding of the bits of coloured glass held up to the light. Much to share that is not necessarily easy to render in a short story format."

— *Montreal Serai*

FORGOTTEN EXILES

FORGOTTEN EXILES

Short Stories

Cyril Dabydeen

Library and Archives Canada Cataloguing in Publication

Title: Forgotten exiles : (short stories) / Cyril Dabydeen.

Other titles: Forgotten exiles (Compilation)

Names: Dabydeen, Cyril, - author.

Identifiers: Canadiana (print) 20240305116 |
  Canadiana (ebook) 20240305159 |

ISBN 9781771617727 (softcover) | ISBN 9781771617734 (PDF) |
ISBN 9781771617758 (Kindle) | ISBN 9781771617741 (EPUB)

Subjects: LCGFT: Short stories.

Classification: LCC PS8557.A25 F67 2024 | DDC C813/.54—dc23

Published by Mosaic Press, Oakville, Ontario, Canada, 2022.

MOSAIC PRESS, Publishers
www.Mosaic-Press.com

Copyright © Cyril Dabydeen, 2024

Cover painting: William Kinnis
Cover design: Amy Land

Printed and bound in Canada

Funded by the Government of Canada
Financé par le gouvernement du Canada | Canadä

ONTARIO
CREATES

MOSAIC PRESS
1252 Speers Road, Units 1 & 2, Oakville, Ontario, L6L 5N9
(905) 825-2130 • info@mosaic-press.com • www.mosaic-press.com

For Alana, Rosemary, and my Family

ALSO BY CYRIL DABYDEEN

TABLE OF CONTENTS

ONE

TWO

THREE

The greatest agony is an untold story.

— Maya Angelou

PART ONE

WELCOMING MR ANANG

Armoured cars kept coming after him in his dream, in his first night in Canada, said Mr Anang, and he'd felt traumatized. Images of Elmina Castle outside Accra also kept being with him, Africans locked up in that horrid place, do you know? I let out an involuntary moan. "Real armoured cars," he repeated. And he'd read about Toronto teenagers going on a visit to Ghana to learn about their African heritage, children of Caribbean-born immigrants. "Why do they?" Mr Anang asked.

I simply shrugged. Now I must revisit the past with him: the role played by Europeans in the slave trade; and the Canadian youngsters coming face-to-face with the horrific images associated with Elmina Castle—dire-looking men and women waiting to be taken across the Atlantic ocean as slaves! *What next?*

"Africans are affronted by such images of Elmina Castle," Mr Anang cried. "Kwame Nkrumah should have torn it down as soon as Ghana became independent!" He heaved in, taking a deep breath.

3

"Elmina Castle's good for the local tourist trade only," he griped, glaring at me. His own Ebbe tribe I must know about with its strong tradition where Christians, Mohameedans (he used that word), and animists live side by side. Then, "People in Ghana still have their fetish beliefs, but the Ebbe people were never in Elmina Castle."

Nothing more...about armoured cars?

And what did I dream about living in Canada for so long? I called myself a *Canadian,* sure.

"What do you really dream about?" Mr Anang insisted to know.

I'd recently dreamt about being in a bus going in many different directions. "What does it mean?" he raised his voice.

"Mean?"

"It means that you have many choices." He wagged a finger at me, his shortish body wavering.

"Really many choices?" I played along.

"Choices in Canada, unlike Africans have."

Armoured cars again, then Elmina Castle and Africans being in the slave ships crossing the ocean. A J.M.W. Turner painting about the slave ship came back to me, I willed myself thinking.

I told Mr Anang how as a young person I'd read books about Africa, including Kwame Nkrumah's *Consciencism,* and about decolonization.

Anang simply talked about the current state of politics in Africa, insisting that Africans needed good governance and partnership-building; it was why he was now in Canada on a World Bank exchange program, I must know. "Real partnership," he sang.

The names of African leaders like Senghor, Nyere, Kenyatta, and Kaunda—the old guard–came back and he flitted his eyes around. Not others like Idi Amin, Bokasa, Mobutu, and Charles Taylor?

Building partnerships with fifty new states that were formed since 1945 was important. *That many?* Mr Anang wasn't getting through to me, it seemed. He dithered.

Now I must know that Nkrumah had married an Egyptian woman mainly because of the necessity to bring sub-Saharan Africa closer to the Arab world. I was eager to know more. "Gamel

4

Nasser loved Nkrumah so much he gave him his daughter's hand; it was quite something," Mr Anang went on.

I'd also read Nkrumah's *Autobiography*, with details of his life in the US, especially about when Nkrumah had been a college student; and after he became Prime Minster of Ghana–formerly Gold Coast–he'd returned to the USA on an official visit with pomp and ceremony, and yes, he'd paid a special visit to his old landlady in Pennsylvania.

Imagine the official state limousine rolling up before the house, and the white landlady ran out to greet him, and embracing him!

Mr Anang looked at me, almost with a fierce will. Then he figured that we had something in common. And how long had I been living in Canada and did I justify calling myself a *Canadian*?

He began telling me about the time he'd spent in the UK, more than a decade ago—when many Ghanaians might have left Africa for good. Yes, leave the animist religion behind, if his Ebbe tribal people mostly who were eager to visit the "mother country". *Why... really?*

"Because Nkrumah became a dictator," Mr Anang rasped.

"See, in England I couldn't find a job, man," he moaned. "They wouldn't even give me a fucking interview." I imagined him nattily attired in kente cloth, authentic Ghanaian style; and, an English inflexion he imitated: "We have no vacancy for you, *mate*"; and so he worked illegally in London in order "to survive". He had to give up his "dignity," ah. When he finally worked in the Earl's Court district of London, the Arab hotel manager underpaid him; he didn't want to give him the tips. *Nothing about Nkrumah marrying an Egyptian woman?*

Mr al-Hajeeb, the hotel manager, said tips were for "services rendered"; and for Arabs it was "No tips, please," which Mr Anang began saying to every new guest at the hotel. Yet all his friends working in the hotel business in London received tips, large tips; even the bell boys got large tips. *Armoured cars again?*

Mr Anang went on: "The Portuguese, the British, all had their holdings of African slaves in Elmina Castle...waiting to be shipped to the New World sugar plantations." Almost collaring me he was, as he asked me to repeat my dream...about the bus going in many different directions here in Canada.

"Must I?" I asked, diminishing before him.

He talked about the special exchange program he was on to help Africans gain "developmental experience," starting with municipal governments. Catch phrases like "civil society" being repeated to him everywhere, Mr Anang said and he grinned. "But development for what, eh?" he scorned. "Is civil society going to make Africans civilized? For real development you must understand people's inner rhythms, including their animist belief!"

I must really know what was causing Africa to be underdeveloped, see. "What?" I asked, my veiled insistence.

The solution was to establish a special School of Management Studies. "A top-level institution is what we need, one like the London School of Economics," Mr Anang sang, and his eyes widened. "A school that emphasizes local conditions and subjective factors only...about a real Africa." I thought about higher institutions already in existence in Ghana, like Makere University; and those other institutions in countries like Nigeria.

"No, no," Mr Anang shook his head. "A school of genuine management, to teach Africans all about ownership and integrity. Africans must be open, be credible and transparent." He again wagged a finger at me. "It'd be one where they teach not only abstract Western theory and philosophy." It was why he'd gone to London in the first place, you see.

Mr Anang faced discrimination, and the fate of the black man in London was a tragedy. He never forgot when a Jamaican immigrant wearing *dread* in London, who was on the dole, demanded his due from the white officials by telling them that his ancestors in Ghana had been shipped from Elmina Castle to work in the Caribbean sugar plantations!

"The Jamaican shouted, 'You been dere, so is why I'm now here, *mon*!'" Mr Anang parodied Jamaican patois: "*See wot de ass I talkin' bout?*"

We both laughed.

Mr Anang revealed that he'd also lived in the Soviet Union where he kept making comparisons with the African way of life between Russians and his own Ebbe people. He'd attended Patrice Lumumba University to learn about a Marxist way of forming partnerships. I called him *tovarish* almost in jest.

He caught on to my humour and laughed. But he was no *comrade*—no *tovarish*. And nothing more about my being in a bus going in different directions? He didn't stay long in Patrice Lumumba University in Moscow, because it only trained Third World students in a materialist way of thinking...during the Cold War.

The word *tovarish* hovered in the air. "I wanted something else for Africa." Mr Anang thumped his chest. Then, "I had a friend who was already there, you know." He twinkled his eyes.

"Not you...alone?" I jibed.

He curled a fist at me. "For real development you have to start with management practices." He opened his mouth wide. "Start with local government and true partnership will come naturally." In Africa...not Russia? But Mr Anang wanted me to talk again about my dream of the bus going in many different directions.

When I didn't, he looked disappointed.

***

Three weeks later I met him once more, and it was his usual mantra about partnership-building: what he'd emphasized to his World Bank benefactors and convincing them to send him to Canada to get first-hand experience. Over the past week he'd been meeting municipal officials to learn about grassroots life in Canada, the rhythm of ordinary people, he called it. "With tropical people you get to know this intuitively; you see their inner soul." Mr Anang had a twinkle in his eyes.

Not how Canadians formed partnerships?

But each Canadian official he'd met so far only described what they were doing, and they used buzz words like "success stories," "best practices," and "transparency." "But these people didn't know about ordinary Canadian people's lives, nothing about their day-to-day existence, and the reality they faced," Mr Anang railed.

7

"This is a big country, with many people living in different regions, with different particularities," he went on. "But, the officials didn't know much about people's inner rhythms."

"D'you mean Native people's rhythms?" I tried.

"Native people and others," he hollered back to me. An Ebbe-African intonation, somewhere.

"What others?" I tried.

"Like those young people in Toronto gone to Ghana to find out about their ancestors kept in Elmina Castle." Yes, *immigrants*, Mr Anang regaled me. Soon it'd be back to his dream of armoured cars, yes.

He described how the Canadian municipal officials had taken him out for lunch and insisted that he must eat everything on his plate. "Why?" he asked them. Did they think everyone in Africa was always so hungry?

He simply told them that when one travelled abroad he must never eat everything on the plate—it was part of his Ebbe custom. Never eat anything bigger than your head too, he emphasized, almost mocking. And his Canadian hosts insisted on giving him a gift—an umbrella.

"Why an umbrella?" he fumed at them.

"Because it rains all the time in Africa," came back at him. *Christ!*

We were both on common ground now because of the symbolism of a tropical downpour, and other images I contrived due to where I'd grown up. "I would really like to travel from coast to coast, to know all about ordinary Canadians," Mr Anang said with new emphasis. "Canadians are a very different people when you get to really know them."

I echoed, "Yes, different."

"You've been living here for more than three decades, not true?"

No immigrant ever became fully adjusted to life in Canada, I told him, like a confession; yes, those immigrants with tropical sensibility tied to their strong sense of themselves. Now I wasn't sure why I said that.

8

Mr Anang eyed me warily. "Canadians may be the happiest people in the world with their high living standard, but...," he said, then stopped suddenly.

He wanted to know if I was happy as an immigrant in Canada. "Are immigrants really happy people here?" He seemed ready to chastise me.

I heaved in, waiting to hear more. "People like you...?" he added, almost bearing down on me. And armoured cars again, if not buses going in many different directions. I hummed something about coping with ice and snow during the long winter months.

Mr Anang laughed, like the laugh was on me.

"Weather one has to cope with wherever you go. Now the harmattan in Africa," he hummed.

Not like the Arctic in Canada? And why did mostly black people keep coming to Canada as refugees in small ramshackle boats, as mentioned in the newspapers? Mr Anang was making me think hard. He resorted to telling me more about life in Britain and Russia, then in Japan; and he talked about Japanese culture. "The Japanese when they say *yes*, they really mean *no*. Asian people are all like that, so polite."

I looked at him doubtfully.

"Their eyes...indeed—it means *no*," he mocked.

Did he see the Asian in me?

In the trains in Tokyo he'd seen people who appeared to have fallen asleep, yet woke up at exactly the right moment when they needed to get off the train. *Imagine that!* "This would never happen in Africa, not in Ghana," Mr Anang sounded exasperated.

"It's the scientific way of people that intrigues me, how they manage their time efficiently," he went on. Indeed it was all about people's rhythms in Japan, Russia, England; and yes, people reading all the time in the train...in London, I must know. "They're so disciplined, the way African people never are.

"In St Petersburg train stations are named after famous writers. Can you ever see that in Africa, a train station named after Chinua Achebe? In Nigeria, a train station named after Nobel Prize winner Wole Soyinka?" he balked.

I made a smirking sound. Imagine a train or bus station in Trinidad named after Nobel Prize winning novelist V.S. Naipaul, or after distinguished poet Derek Walcott. *Go on, tell him.*

"We need to erect pillars of wisdom," Mr Anang declared, "to help our people develop a new way of thinking, for them to aim for high standards, social and economic." Marxist socialism wouldn't teach him that? "Pillars of wisdom across Africa, more than just concrete high-rises," he glowered. "It's not only about foreign aid, getting alms... as some missionaries want us to believe."

I became a little frightened by Mr Anang. He was warming up to armoured cars again in Canada. He said that partnership means *friendship*. "It's our folk tradition, what's within us, my Ebbe people especially."

I sucked in more air.

"But what kind of partnership do I see here? They put me in an office to sit before a computer all day, so I could look at what's written on the screen. Then it's talk about measuring this and measuring that, and they call it accountability and transparency, not partnership." Mr Anang tightened his lips.

In the same small office he was in, he often fell asleep; and how he longed to be with his own Ebbe people. He related the story of a Canadian official who'd been sent to visit Ghana and how he'd been treated by the locals as he travelled around the villages in an exchange program. "People welcomed him everywhere, he was overwhelmed by African people's hospitality. It's the tradition...to make this Canadian feel like one of us. This official never saw such hospitable people anywhere before, animists mostly," said Mr Anang coming closer to me, the *Asian*.

In a washroom in Kumasi the official had looked at himself in the mirror, and he was surprised to see a black face...not his own white face staring back at him. Mr Anang burst out laughing. *Do I know?*

Now what kind of face did I see in the mirror here in Canada?

"You've been living here long enough...what kind of face?" he demanded to know. I hadn't thought about it like this before, I told him.

He snickered, "The Canadian official really wanted his face to be black...which was why he came to Africa." Whimsical he sounded. He paused. Then: "Maybe you will see yourself with only a white face if you stay longer in Canada."

It sounded like a threat, almost a forewarning. He went on about those Africans being sent abroad by the World Bank— some who quickly spent their per diem, which was almost a year's salary in Ghana. "They kept buying lots of gifts for their relatives—which white people never do. It has something to do with management practices, no?" Mr Anang asked.

Silence...between us for a while. Then to Elmina Castle once more...with the image of armoured cars. He'd recently read that the Danes had also been slave traders as Mr Anang insisted that I know. He moaned again, as he almost frightened me.

***

I waited to hear more about the officials he met in Ottawa who made him sit before a computer in an office all day, one without a window, so he couldn't look out to see real Canadians. Yes, for him not to get a sense of people's lives with their inner rhythms.

But in Africa if he had such an office he would see friends and relatives coming and going, without anyone having to make an appointment, Mr Anang said. "It's our folk tradition," he announced.

He dared me to disagree with him. "Does Canada have a folk tradition?"

Again he talked about forming genuine partnerships, and not for him to sit long hours before a computer where he kept yawning all the time. Then, "How many choices d'you really have here in Canada?"

Elmina Castle still with me, and the young students from Canada actually in Ghana... as I imagined being with them; and maybe I was still dreaming. I also saw my face in a mirror in Kumasi, Ghana; but not in Canada...with a white face only.

Mr Anang grinned, thinking he was getting to me. But it was sitting before a computer in an Ottawa office and thinking about forming partnerships that riled him, and yes, imagining devils and witchcraft in the animist tradition far more than an Ebbe's fetish he had to deal with. *Like what I must really know.*

* * *

In my next dream I thought it would be about my encountering a lookalike Mr Anang—one who kept comparing African life with Canadian life. More faces...came to me, and people with their inner rhythms most of all. Suddenly it became my strong urge to travel across Canada—going from one town to another in province after province. Odd, I also saw myself in Japan watching people getting on and off trains; and in Russia and England, too...seeing people reading all the time, the way Africans never did.

That same night I woke up with a start, perspiring heavily. And unconsciously I longed for that bus in my dream once more. But this time the bus was stuck in one place; and I was the bus driver. *Go on, tell Mr Anang.* A grin spread across his flat face; then he laughed.

The image of students in Toronto visiting Elmina Castle also came back, and the Jamaican in London berating the British officials in patois.

Yes, everything being so authentic and to be experienced as I began telling Mr Anang...with our coming closer, much closer—if only because of the sustained Asian in me: how far... or, how near.

CHRISTINE, INTERRUPTED

A pressing action against her shoulder Christine felt when the youth jostled her, and her watch was gone—pulled from her wrist, just like that. Immediately she reached out to Immanuel; but he shrugged and said, *"Think nothing of it!"* And see, the watch had been given to her by her mother when she was thirteen which she'd kept fingering in the plane coming over to Kenya.

Did Immanuel really say *Think nothing of it?*

Nairobi's crowded streets, the jangly noise, tintinnabulation: market-sellers, hawkers everywhere. Kenya was no different from other parts of the Third World, she figured. Now pain on her mother's face, a mother who died two years ago, Christine visualized. She wiped perspiration from her neck, arms, determined not to give in to sentiment over the loss of the watch. But now returning to Africa was making Immanuel moody.

"Hey, Momma!" someone called out. *Momma?*

"You...white momma!"

The wiry-looking youth with acetylene eyes: Did he think Christine was *American*?

"Momma!"

Christine steeled herself not to react, as a *Canadian*. She gripped Immanuel's hand. The humidity was viscous, so unlike being in her accustomed northern hemisphere. Tell that to this particular youth who kept calling out to her. And maybe Immanuel was feeling uncomfortable escorting her around, almost as if wanting her to experience how it actually felt being a "foreigner" as he'd complained about in Ottawa.

Christine hoped for a better relationship between them, you see; and so much *she* wanted to come to Africa. It'd been six years ago when she nearly visited Ghana as part of a group of volunteer-aid workers wanting to learn about self-development in the former Gold Coast. She'd researched facts about the Ashanti people, and where slavery first started. Were slaves really brought to the New World from this region of West Africa?

Think nothing of it! came back to her.

She'd read Kwame Nkrumah's autobiography, the only work on Africa she'd found in the local library, and tried to imagine what she would really see in Ghana. But the trip's organizers suddenly called it off. She'd cried for two whole days after.

Immanuel simply said she would get over it; and she would have felt "displaced" in Africa anyhow. *Really displaced?* He, a former diplomat's son, used to a life of privilege. But his family had recently come upon hard times, and he often talked about his father's "displacement," as stated in the official government letter.

Christine had first met Immanuel in a small café-bar on the university campus in Ottawa, and she immediately felt something click between them. "I'm from Kenya," he said, introducing himself.

"Oh?"

Ghana...Gambia...Kenya.

"You must come with me to Africa one day," he said with a smile. Yes, just like that. Immanuel's charm, ah. Sure, and she told him about research she'd done on slavery, and about her dwelling

14

on Elmina Castle in Ghana. *Think...nothing of it?* Yes, Immanuel's eyes had glimmered. Studying law he was while working part-time as a security guard, and being sent around from one government building to another in the cold winter months.

How he hated it! But part-time work gave him ample time to study, and to think about his relatives in Kenya, he said. Christine wanted to know how his father's tribe was being targeted, and how people became victims of the government program of "realignment," as he'd told her.

"You're really very keen about Africa," he said, looking into her eyes. And she read the letters he showed her. And since "returning" from Ghana she would become defensive about Africa, especially when her white Canadian friends said anything negative about the "dark continent," as some still called it.

Her actually being here now in Kenya—eastern Africa indeed. And the market noise in Nairobi...so far from Canada. *"Momma!"* A flamboyante tree came in her line of vision, the leaves eaten by giraffes, and elephants pulling whole branches down. A safari she'd wanted to go on. But Immanuel wanted nothing to do with safaris.

"My watch is gone," she said to him in a wry way.

Immanuel talked about when his father had been a diplomat in the Soviet Union and he'd lived with the family and studied at the People's Free University in Moscow. Christine had to almost pry this information out of him. And she remembered how in Ottawa he'd gotten into a spat with the university authorities when a female administrative staff picked on him. *Because he was from Africa?*

He'd yelled at the staff, calling the woman a Communist. He had to spend the night in an Ottawa jail—just for that? Christine stayed up late being anxious about him, waiting for his phone call. But he didn't want to get her involved, he told her. "I'm a Canadian," she'd said to him.

"So...?"

"I could have helped, I know how the system works."

"You do...the system?"

"I was born here!"

15

Immanuel became defensive. "I was just embarrassed, that's all."

"To be put in jail? You're not in the Soviet Union, you know." Why she said that she wasn't sure.

"I'm from Kenya, an African," he answered her defensively. Then, "Christ, I yelled at the university people. The woman laughed at me. A black woman at that, from the West Indies. What do West Indians know about Africa anyway?"

Christine had done some research on the West Indies and read a book by an eminent historian, Walter Rodney, who was born in British Guiana. Was that country part of the West Indies? Slavery from Africa— did it extend everywhere...and to Brazil and other parts of that large southern continent? How little did she know!

Immanuel had begun to resent her "motherly" ways—as she became protective of him because, well, he was from the "dark continent"? "Come with me to Africa," he finally said to her. "You want to see my family, don't you?"

"I do."

"Then come..."

Immanuel's family had been phoning and writing letters for months urging him to come home. Some relatives were becoming sick, one letter said, and about a strange illness sweeping across the countryside, dengue fever. Not, well...political sickness? When another letter came, it really started affecting their relationship.

Immanuel talked about the personal commitment he'd made to his family, many living some distance from Nairobi in a small village. Not to his father only? *Think nothing of it.*

Where was the youth who'd snatched the watch from her wrist? Somewhere in the crowd looking at her with a smirk on his face? Christine heaved in. Immanuel simply looked at her with a stoic expression. *Think nothing of it.*

***

She wanted to understand Immanuel's family customs, their tradition especially. He said she might have only an anthropologist's interest in Africa. Tell him she'd never finished college, but had read anthropologist Margaret Mead; and yes, she was turned off by Mead's sometimes patronizing ways about Africans.

Christine didn't want to be labelled having an interest in Africa as a white person with liberal guilt. She was also coping with her own parents' conservative views. Her father's awkward silence, she remembered, when she'd told him on the phone that she had an *African* boyfriend. See, her parents still considered her the "baby" of the family, though she was now in her thirties.

The image of her mother's watch as an heirloom came back to her and she let out an involuntary moan. Immanuel hummed, "Don't worry...."

"Oh?"

Odd, she began feeling strangely glad the watch was gone; it never carried the right time anyway. "Hey Momma"...the tug at her wrist once more. Poverty no doubt forced people to do strange things—the crimes being committed in Africa. But in Canada this could have also happened, she figured.

She thought about her own lower middle-class family background; but it was a family that worked hard as her father often said to her. She really wanted to take Immanuel to meet her parents, her father especially. "Why...what for?" Immanuel balked.

"For them to get to know you."

"To see what I look like, that I am not...?"

"Not what?"

"A Communist," he grimaced. "Can't I be just as I am... as we are? I don't have to meet them, you know."

"They are my parents, Immanuel," she agonized.

Maybe it was his anxiety about how they would react to him, and for him to find out that not all white people are racists? *Tell him*!

Eventually Immanuel agreed to meet her parents at the farm outside of Peterborough, Ontario. And he helped her father chop wood. But the two men hardly said a word to each other. Her mother, Greta, muttered, "What's with him?"

"With who?"

Christine knew her mother meant her father, who was suffering from prostate cancer; and her mother had a weak heart.

Christine instinctively looked at her wrist for the watch as her mind flitted back to Ottawa, then to Immanuel's friends who would argue about Africa's fate, as some called it. Immanuel had mostly African friends, some in their own racially mixed relationships, like Marcia—also from Kenya; and the talk about cultures and Swahili lore with visits to Marcia's home in Lowertown drifted back...to Christine. Emile, Marcia's husband—a French-Canadian—would be dourly quiet.

Then Christine decided to take a course on cross-cultural training.

But Immanuel was cynical: "What do you need a course for?" He forced a laugh. Marcia and the others laughed too, because of what they figured might be taught in such a course...by a white instructor, with lots of sociology-talk.

"What...for?" Christine looked at Immanuel; and she might have wanted to inform the class about her relationship with him.

"It's only about Africa, you know," Marcia had said with a grin.

Immanuel again shrugged. *Think nothing of it.*

***

His eyes, like embers; and the one youth might have been surprised by the pain he saw on Christine's face. "Yes...you, white momma!" Immanuel made a scoffing noise about the heat, and the tropical stickiness that Christine found so irritating, though outside of Nairobi it was less so; in the city the concrete kept the humidity in, Immanuel told her. But he too was finding it unbearable, because he'd lived in Canada for so long? Yeah, he'd become acclimatized.

Now being in Africa ...maybe it was the break she needed from still grieving for her mother who had died. Christine's mind wandered...far. It would be an occasion to meet Immanuel's parents, though the family's problems were causing him great stress. *Not get help from the Canadian development agency called CIDA?*

Immanuel lamented that his father was now only a small-town official who worked far from the village in "staff realignment"

18

after having served the country so well, especially in the former Soviet Union.

"Hey, Momma," Christine heard again.

An image of Ghana's Elmina Castle, somewhere. Not Mombasa with its beach-side resort! Immanuel looked around anxiously. And Christine's emotions seemed mixed with a strange guilt...of actually being in poverty-stricken Africa. Soon she'd be going past Kusumu to Immanuel's village on the western coast—she'd prepared herself for it.

"You sure?" he asked.

"Sure...?"

"We could stay in Kusumu, or in a hotel in Nairobi."

"We've been through that before."

"This is no cross-culturalism course, you know."

She looked at him with a grimace.

"I mean, you now being literally in Africa." He too grimaced.

A clicking noise she heard, like from the one who'd stolen her watch and had stuck his tongue out at her. Christine rubbed her eyes. Was the youth really here at the bus stop...to bid her goodbye?

They entered a rickety bus after waiting for almost two hours. Jostling amidst distinct smells as the bus trundled along, going full speed, then rolling over bumpy road. Immanuel gritted his teeth.

Why did he want to live in Canada anyway?

It was what Christine's father had asked him when they'd chopped wood together. The bus sped along. A Massai woman in the front seat with a chicken in her lap with the legs tied together Christine looked at; she feared the chicken would suddenly spring loose, and no one would be able to stop it!

Immanuel didn't want to go on about the treatment his father received at the hands of the government, he told her...amidst voices with quaint accents tied to Swahili jabber all around in the bus. Christine was now really far from home—Canada and Kenya being worlds apart. *But no more?*

She really looked forward to meeting genuine local people in Kusumu. Immanuel bit into a mango with relish. Christine did too, slurping a little. They observed the friendly faces in the bus, Kikuyu mostly. The women outside wearing garish cotton dresses with floral patterns who hailed at them, hands flailing. But one or two others looked critically at Christine. The bus's jangly noise rose. A lone male elephant trundled along the road...somewhere. Now almost voiceless Christine felt.

A little past Kusumu they got off and walked a short distance on a patchy red brick road. Kids ran towards them, as Immanuel enthusiastically called out their names. Did one of them say, "Hey Momma"? Bright-eyed kids with stringy bodies, some pretending to be long or middle distance runners. But others looked despondent. Christine had read about kwashiorkor, bloated bellies.

One young girl tagged along close to her. Immanuel looked back.

"Are you okay?" he asked.

"Yes," Christine replied.

"You sure?"

"Just tired."

Village elders came as Christine and Immanuel walked along with some family members. She had on the cotton dress she'd especially bought for the occasion. Now she wanted to talk to everyone despite the language barrier. How the children laughed with their flashing white teeth and broad smiles.

Christine kept being "humble and friendly," as Immanuel teased her about. He seemed unlike how he was in Canada, ah. They ate corn meal, *ugali*, a special porridge. Christine found it suited her stomach well. Immanuel always liked it since as a kid, he said.

"You...all Luo people?" Christine asked an elder with large, somnolent-looking eyes.

"We are."

"Everyone?"

She squatted with the older women. The men gawked, standing by themselves. Immanuel said he would soon have to go off for a few days to meet some relatives in other villages, and Christine could remain behind. "Momma, momma," she heard again. Yes, her mother's watch was really gone!

"Mosquitoes like me," she said casually to the village women swatting flies around her. The men looked at her impassively.

Night again, but she couldn't easily sleep, though she figured she would get used to the humidity. Immanuel too couldn't sleep, he told her. Did he want to, well, hurry back to Canada? They stayed in a dwelling adjacent the main house. There was an outhouse that didn't stink much. Dogs yapped. Cocks crowed early in the morning.

Christine enjoyed the plantain and goat meat cooked by Immanuel's mother. She helped with cutting and peeling cassava, then pounded it to make *fufu*. "Always be humble and friendly," Christine hummed to herself. The others again laughed.

When Immanuel returned after three days away, he said his brother was really ill. His mother appeared quiet. Immanuel said they could go to Tanzania, which wasn't as developed as Kenya. To Uganda, too. Oh, not Mombasa?

Christine wanted to travel much more. And go to Ghana next!

See, Africa was such a large continent. She remembered the instructor of the cross-culturalism course in Ottawa urging everyone to read Conrad's *Heart of Darkness*. Not read Chinua Achebe or Wole Soyinka, genuine African authors as Immanuel wanted her to do? Read Walter Rodney too, the African-Guyanese historian! And there was novelist Ngugi wa thiong'o.

Immanuel talked about family disputes he must try to settle; he had to leave the village once more for a day or two. "What disputes?" Christine asked. He wouldn't say. What if he was betrothed to a girl in the next village, which custom demanded? Would the elders tell Christine? She thought about her mother's watch again.

More village women came around. "What is it?" one asked, noting her sullen mood. Christine shook her head.

"Tell...me," came back at her.

"I have a headache," Christine lied, pointing to the sun.

She thought about her mother more and more, and about her father living alone outside of Peterborough on his farm with a dog that was old and becoming gnarly. She missed her father very much. *Tell them!*

Funny that she was thinking about this here in Africa with mangy mongrels moving around her. She wished she could spend more time with her father; she did.

Nothing being said about a native girl Immanuel might be seeing in the next village? *No-no-no,* cried Immanuel's mother. And what did her father and Immanuel really talk about when they chopped wood together at the Peterborough farm? Christine tried to make light of everything with her unaffected laughter.

Imagine telling Marcia about this when she returned to Ottawa. Maybe Marcia would say "There isn't much to learn from them, you know." "But I did learn...something!"

Like what?

That *cross-culturalism* was just a made-up word.

***

Three weeks went by quickly. Christine and Immanuel were set to return to Canada just when she wanted to learn more about the Luo people: their tribe, and more about the culture. She'd begun seeing Immanuel's family in their *native* ways. Then Immanuel suddenly said they shouldn't leave just yet.

"Why not?" she asked.

"There's more for me to do here."

"Remember your studies that you have to complete in Canada."

"That can wait...for later."

"But you want to practice law one day...in Africa."

"Not anymore."

Immanuel was really worried about his father because the government was sending him to another district far from Kusumu as part of the "realignment," Christine learnt.

"Momma, Momma!" Local kids kept coming around her, some with kwashiorkor, bloated bellies. Others with largish eyes popping out of their heads, almost exophthalmos. Did they think Christine wanted to hurry Immanuel back to Canada?

Marcia somewhere in the background: "Just like Africans to think," and laughed.

Christine summoned another image: of her father chopping wood, and the old dog yapping. Immanuel might have asked her father something about Communism, thinking of what he might be interested in. Not ask Immanuel if he was a Muslim?

Christine genuinely wanted to feel she belonged in Africa: first in Ghana... now in Kenya, east or west coast–which she could boast about later. *Really boast in Canada.* She also wanted to talk to Immanuel's father, not just his mother, and ask him about life in the new Kenya developing, and his views about the former Soviet Union. *Did she?*

Immanuel grew more anxious.

Christine pictured him back in Ottawa doing his part-time job and looking so ridiculous in his security-guard uniform. She reflected on why she'd never continued with university herself; she had taken only three courses; but she didn't want to compete with kids just out of high school half her age and really good with computers. Immanuel looked at her quizzically. *Think nothing of it?*

***

Their airline flight home couldn't be changed in Nairobi after the last phone call to the travel agency. It was their final night in the concrete building they stayed in, an oblong shed that seemed to grow longer each day. Christine said she liked being in the Kusumu village as she looked up at the African night sky with the large moon, which she never saw the likes of in Canada.

Here too, it was her lack of awareness of skin-colour; and she'd chided Immanuel not to think much about race and identity—for it didn't really matter at all. *It does*, he rebutted.

She closed her eyes. *What now?*

"What?"

Looking out from the plane's window Christine felt she was indeed leaving Africa for good; and yes, leaving Immanuel's village just when she was getting familiar with the customs, and learning more about African people's ways. And Immanuel had met his father, finally...to hear him bemoan his fate, and about his time in the Soviet Union. *Really that?* Christine fell asleep.

She was jolted awake. "Momma!" she heard.

Immanuel also opened his eyes; and maybe he hoped to see his father waving to him, though *realigned.* All the while Christine kept being humble and friendly, what her mother had really urged her to be in Africa. And the sound of her father chopping wood in a flurry of strokes, yes—with Immanuel doing the same alongside him...as the two men casually talked to each other about life in Africa.

Talk about Communism, too?

Her mother's watch—timeless as it was. Christine held Immanuel's hand. Cirrus clouds moved swiftly, then a cluster of cumulus dragged by in her line of vision. The plane kept moving along, and a whole continent disappearing, oh. She rubbed her eyes, unconsciously listening for the one youth's voice yet calling her *momma.*

But only a silent clamour came...like a giant heart beating; which Immanuel also heard; and the sound closing in on them. Instinctively Christine looked at her wrist for the watch. *Think nothing of it!*

WEST MEETS EAST

S heer happenstance it seemed when I met Sanderson again; and the years didn't matter anymore with our being here. A glance, a turnaround, at the airport in this northern capital city. Exit or entry points before me, I figured. But Sanderson immediately looked away, he didn't want to be recognized. *By...me?* When I'd last seen him at the College almost a decade ago he was given to ennui or desultoriness. A certain mystery about him there was, I believed. And something else, too, between us...if because of my being an *outsider.*

Bald-looking he now was when he'd once had a full head of hair; hair meant everything to him then. His pate shone. And he used to move around campus with one female or another: first, with Clara from "the islands," Bermuda, then another from Belize, and one from somewhere in Central America who literally held on to Sanderson's shirtsleeves as they walked along. With each new female he drifted to another exotic place. *Where...next?*

Then came a fallow period when Sanderson had been given to muttering to himself, so strange. Fergus, a teaching colleague, with bluster, would heckle Sanderson who became the butt of our jokes. "Look at him," another colleague scoffed upon seeing Sanderson escorting another female. *How...exotic!*

"Yeah," Fergus grinned.

It all stemmed from Sanderson reading the likes of Somerset Maugham, Graham Greene, Evelyn Waugh, and Joseph Conrad. A genuine heart-of-darkness...and his being a special teacher, nothing less. Not what Fergus ever imagined, ah. Worlds now close up as I looked at him. Here at the Ottawa airport Sanderson dithered, looking around.

I was returning from Louisiana with Bayou culture in me: vodou and famed Marie Laveau, if you must know. New Orleans' French Quarter, long before Hurricane Katrina. I waited for my suitcase to come tumbling down the carousel. Sanderson was looking for *someone* who might have been in the plane with me. He averted his eyes. Passengers kept grabbing their luggage, in a scrimmage. New Orleans with gators yet with me, ah.

Sanderson crinkled his eyes when a short, hefty woman came forward. Dark-hued, hair cascading down to her waist—someone from Bangladesh, maybe. A handsome blonde boy jutted out from her arms; his sandy-and peach-coloured hair an unsettled-looking bundle. He pulled, tugged, excited to be here in Ottawa. He...with his mother.

Sanderson quickly moved towards them, taking light steps; nothing jaunty about him. The hefty-bodied mother barked an order at the boy. Sanderson instinctively fussed over him. *He...the boy's father?*

The hefty woman became aware of me looking at them.

Impulsively Sanderson grabbed the boy's arm. But the eight-year-old dashed to another tumble of suitcases at the carousel. I immediately thought of the Vietnam War and the kids fathered by American GI's and left behind to fend for themselves. A movie-maker's image, imprinted in my mind. Sanderson was having this effect on me.

The mother again fussed; and the boy was the result of her union with Sanderson no doubt. The College teaching days returned with Fergus being at it. Bruno, Harold, and other teaching colleagues snickered. I waited for my own suitcase to come tumbling down the carousel.

Sanderson simmered. The image of him with his last female companion sauntering along the College corridor persisted with me.

Continents coming closer. Bangladesh's monsoon, and whole villages floating away because of a recent cyclone. The mangrove-laden Sundarbans, and rivers overflowing their banks. Boats capsized. Ah, water cascaded down the Ganges River from the Himalayas. The Bangladeshi woman's hair with tresses jiggled and swayed as she pulled at her son, like pulling his arm out. Religious strife and clashes between Hindus and Muslims in the subcontinent. Tribals, mountain and hill peoples without their natural rights, which activist-author Arundhati Roy had railed about.

Had it been ten years since I left the College? Sanderson patted his pate; gangly he looked. The woman was squat-looking. The boy let out a squeal. *Ooohh-aaaah!* Sanderson panicked, but turned around and glared...at me? He once more reached out to grab the boy's arm. But the boy knocked it off, like swatting away at a fly.

"Hi!" cried the mother. "Hi!" the boy hissed back.

"Hi-hi-hi!" she railed.

Onlookers at the airport sniggered. Sanderson's lips throbbed.

"Hi," he seethed inwardly. He might have first met this woman in one of his English classes—and the "twain" meeting. Sanderson was finished with the Caribbean and Latin America. South Asia was now in his sights. "Hi," Sanderson yet fussed over the boy.

The Bangladeshi woman smiled at me, as if aware of me, my prescience. Sanderson stood abjectly apart...beside her. The others at the College in former days: Fergus, a math lecturer, who'd said, "Why doesn't Sanderson travel abroad if he's so taken by these women?" *Foreign...women?*

27

"Why doesn't he?" Bruno grated.

Marian, another teaching colleague, with English airs, who'd once been to South Africa and bemoaned the apartheid system, made a face. *Now at me!* Sanderson, as was his manner, drifted in and out of his office—like in an experiment in "living existentially," he called it. His clothes-horse was a pushed-back corner-space; a couch was his bed at *night*. He showered at the College gym and ate in the cafeteria. Fergus skeptically asked, "Does he really sleep there?"

"How could he?" another chimed.

The campus was his own sprawling, but marked-out, space. The College newspaper talked about an education-drive and a campaign to reach out to the world, which Sanderson no doubt took seriously. A Canadian city, well, now a much talked-about international centre. Sanderson carried out his "experiment" in new-age living. New Orleans with me—like a counterpoint.

The blonde boy again hurled himself around. Sanderson fretted.

A real game was on! The long-haired woman despaired of her son.

Sanderson balked.

"Hi, hi!" the boy shouted.

Sanderson was out of his depth with the boy. His "wife" whirled around, laughing embarrassedly.

Other "passengers" also laughed at the drama unfolding.

The woman and the boy were now like two kids chasing each other around the carousels. The airport diminished in size. When the boy yelped again, onlookers applauded. Planes droned in the background.

Sanderson eyed me, ruefully. Instinctively I moved close... to him.

Recognize me? "Sanderson," I said mutely.

The boy squealed and dashed through a group of tie-and-jacket-attired passengers, bureaucrats all. The mother's lips convulsed. Everyone seemed awe-struck as she tried to cope with her son.

Sanderson was hapless-looking.

More boats capsized in a Bangladesh river not far from Calcutta: all of Bengali India, Pakistan. The Hooghly River, then the Brahmaputra, coming down the Himalayas during monsoon season. The Ganges River with holiness...as devout worshippers eyed us from afar. Mother-goddess Kali, slant-eyed: *Watch out!*

The boy glared...at me. The mother kept her hands akimbo. Vietnam ...close-up.

The mother knitted her eyelashes. Time for Sanderson's full recognition of me, as I was yet riveted to the boy. American GI's leaving Vietnam...and the Vietcong taking over; the Eurasian kids left behind to face the Communists' wrath in Saigon. This boy's undaunted spirit here in the North surprised me.

"Hi," the mother wailed, "come back here!"

The boy wagged his tongue out at her. He dared Sanderson to come at him, too. Bags, more luggage, tumbled down the carousels. Ski equipment and boxes with skates clunked. Winter in a cold Ottawa a-coming. The Rideau Canal invited everyone to skate in the longest rink of the world.

Monsoon winds prevailed. Bangladesh's typhoon a counterpoint once more. "Hi, hi!" came a further wail. The boy was determined to survive. Wind slashed against his face. Fergus grinned. Bruno blustered with a guffaw. Unconsciously Sanderson's hand went to his pate. "You," he said.

Me?

The boy laughed again, gloating. The crowd cheered...like at a hockey game in a wayside rink. Fergus and the others now at the airport vicariously observing everything, like a predicted side-show. The College doors opened, closed. Planes...in a far sky...the tropics near the equator. Where now New Orleans with gators?

I shrugged. Sanderson looked hard at me. Closer...north.

Could the boy intuitively tell about us? Sanderson simmered. *Calling... Vietnam.* Comedic movie-actor Robin Williams' radio voice now really highpitched, ah.

***

The boy tapped me on the hand as he thought I'd drifted off; even as New Orleans and Lake Pontchartrain lingered somewhere in the background. Sanderson yet averted his eyes, not looking at me. The Bangladeshi woman appeared almost tall, oh.

"You," the boy accosted.

I was tongue-tied. Sanderson dithered. "Hi-hi!" the boy hissed again. He wasn't just a boy, but almost a man, if seeming like a thirteen-year-old. Another moment he was younger, eight or nine.

His mother smiled.

Did Sanderson not want me to know that the boy was his son? The ring on the woman's finger. And a similar ring Sanderson wore, yes. The boy's "Hi-hi" diverted my attention once more. I tried to reply...as the mother forced me to recognize her.

Really...you?

Sanderson grew more uncomfortable. *We're indeed here.* The wife smiled coyly. The boy touched my hand with strange affection. *Imagine, eh.* The image of Sanderson escorting another exotic-looking woman on campus, if with Caribbean Clara once more. The equator came much closer. Jungly forests...alongside prairie tundra. Fergus and the others applauded.

"Hi, hi!" I unconsciously let out.

Then a more melodic "Hoi, hoi!" Witchery of a kind. Past days with vodou queen Marie Laveau. Gulf of Mexico waters nearer. Lobster and jumbo shrimp jumped up and down in a spasm. *Tell Sanderson.* Marie Laveau with Lake Pontchartrain. Silhouettes...as men and women danced around a boiling cauldron, then began throwing live chickens into it, and women—mostly white—linking hands with Marie Laveau and her group of males, all chanting *Hoi! Hoi!*

Sanderson and his wife were also there in New Orleans with me. The boy whooped it up louder, "Hoi, hoi!" Sanderson dared me to keep being at it. The boy's nails dug in.

Suitcases hurtled down the carousels with more distinct thuds. Clunk-clunk! Sanderson raised his head. And where did he first meet her, this woman with her long tresses? She whirled into more cascades...as rivers overflowed their banks and boats capsized with people and livestock kept struggling to survive.

The sandy-haired boy was a born survivor, I figured. *Good morning...Vietnam!*

***

Sanderson would be gone from the College for good, if only from the likes of Bruno and Fergus; and I would remain in the north...as planes landed, and then departed. The carousels kept being busier than usual as more suitcases tumbled down, here like no other airport in the world.

Sanderson turned at an angle and made as if to come towards me.

The boy suddenly laughed. But Sanderson walked past me. The boy's laughter grew louder. The woman with her long tresses nodded.

Sanderson took his cue from her, and he too nodded. To me?

A longer distance, in the boy's eyes. "Hoi! Hoi!" Voices came from everywhere...calling out. Involuntarily I looked around.

The woman indeed came towards me. Recognition of a new place, in a new time...not unlike what Sanderson expected from me. Odd I imagined Bruno, Fergus, and the others instinctively applauding. Worlds coming closer.

MY TEACHING DAYS

M y teaching days were numbered, and I'd started looking at my colleagues with suspicion with the sense of my unique beginning, in a manner of speaking. The new class before me, students who were grown adults, *Caterers*—makers of pastries. But taking English was compulsory for them here at the college; and I figured they disliked being in an English class, these students. And the advice given to me: "Go easy on them"—a directive from the Department Head.

"Easy?"

"Do they know what's ahead for them?" one colleague grated. Another simply laughed.

I surveyed the students whose ages ranged from eighteen to twenty-five, and a far place in my mind with origins I cultivated, believe me. And before long, one particular student stood out: Yves, French-Canadian by the looks of it. He was most likely in the wrong course, wrong class, he would do much better in a humanities-academic stream at a large university—an Ivy League school. I imagined him poring over tomes, classical literature and philosophy being his forte, and becoming acquainted with the likes of Descartes, Rousseau, Voltaire, Hegel...Foucault. Definitely not pastry-making. *Let who eat cake?*

Yves shrugged.

He knew what I was thinking, it seemed. The others grinned, one or two mockingly. And after the first week I'd begun accepting them for who they were, if only because everything was commonplace, or mundane.

Mike, the tallest in the class, gawky-looking, leered at me. He was called a "lunatic" by the others as they grinned. "I am just an Anglophone," he hummed. "We're all lunatics here," guffawed another.

Mike simply shrugged his large frame, jaw dropping noticeably.

The girls–women really–made faces. *At me?* Meeka, large-hipped, blithely said her boyfriend had moved out west to Calgary, and she would join him out there later. She casually asked if I was single; and did she want to "fix me up" with a friend?

Some friend. The friend was having a party, and I was invited; her friend had two kids, I must know. *Sure!* Meeka giggled again. I encouraged informality, like my new teaching strategy. *Yes, go easy on them.*

Yves glanced at me. No longer Ivy League potential?

"Thank you," I said to Meeka.

When I didn't show up at the party, she said her friend was disappointed. Caril, sitting next to Meeka, made a long face— Mona Lisa-like. Stubie, a sturdy male, plonked himself down next to Caril; he thought he was God's gift to the human race, grated another female. Stubie smirked.

Caril remained indifferent, but pretended loyalty to him. Stubie had eyes for Caril, everyone knew. But Caril was plain-looking, Meeka had said; she had a strange way with guys like Stubie, and it was weird.

The class before me, and I kept being aware of Caril more than usual as she looked at me intently, maybe thinking of the big writing assignment ahead; and yes, the essay she would hand in since she was past doing functional English; her talents were beyond being a caterer, see.

Caril yawned when I mentioned one of the greats of literature. Shakespeare: sure, and she nodded. Why then I sensed she might have read everything the Elizabethan bard wrote I didn't know. Sitting next to her, Stubie opened his mouth wide, hippopotamus-wide.

Other students guffawed. Often playful, they were.

Yves, well, was stone-silent. Meeka laughed again, and others laughed with her, Doug and Robin especially—the latter long-boned, a broom handle.

I informed them that they all had to give short talks, an "Oral" assignment, as part of the course curriculum. But they hated "public-speaking." *Who doesn't?* Mike blurted out, "What's really Oral?"

Meeka's entire body throbbed. "Christ, we're just caterers," she snapped. Others repeated what Meeka said, like instant cheerleaders.

"I know," I hummed.

But in truth I liked listening to students' orals when I could simply observe them more closely, and maybe appreciate their hidden talent. *What hidden talent?*

My teaching colleagues sniffed, ah.

Mike droned on, "What's Oral—tell us!"

After class Meeka came and leaned near me, cheek by jowl. Her street-smarts I must cope with. Stubie immediately flexed his muscles; and he always wanted female attention. Caril cast her eyes on him ruefully. Mike drew alongside and dwarfed me, asking for advice on his Oral assignment. Tense he looked.

Why not speak on his speciality: something about the food industry, like pastry-making? I patronized him, and he knew it. "No," Mike quaked, glaring at me.

I glared back at him.

The others snickered; but not Yves.

"No-no," sang Mike, with an abjectly blank stare.

One teaching colleague hooted, "They're just caterers, what's the point?" But I ignored this. A foreign place or instinct still in me, like an escape point.

Mike badgered me about his Oral: he was taking it more seriously than the others. Yves was solemn. I looked at him; and he looked back at me without blinking. Robin, well, chortled.

"What d'you intend to talk about, Yves?" I tried.

"Talk about?"

"Your Oral assignment."

Mike's facial muscles twitched, capillaries stretched.

"What?" Yves looked blankly at me, and maybe he was hard-of-hearing. His body grew elongated. He muttered something about another Quebec referendum in the making with politicians everywhere being at it on radio talk-shows, TV; and maybe he couldn't fool me about his loyalty.

Did the others think Yves was a separatist because of his being Quebecois? *Pierre Vallieres*, let them know who he was. *Really who?*

Yves was all for the Quiet Revolution, make no mistake about it. He talked in class about the "French fact," like something arcane or bizarre, and mysterious he sounded, then inevitably...about Rene Levesque. The nineteen-eighties kept changing, evolving in me.

I asked where I was going as a Canadian. *Really Canadian?* "Quebec mustn't separate," Mike snapped, jaw hung low. "What for," he growled, "we're all Canadians!"

"Are we?" Yves hissed back.

One or two others looked around with gawky stares. Muffled applause, everyone being in agreement with Mike...or Yves. A collective instinct I murmured to myself; and it didn't matter where I came from with "my foreign roots"—with my own sense of *solitude*.

Meeka tittered in a sudden spasm. Mike hummed louder under his breath. I might have *motivated* him about his Oral. "What's your topic for the assignment going to be?" I asked Mike again, and he dreaded the question. He dwarfed me by coming closer.

I hated being dwarfed. Caril leaned forward, her thin body stretching, coming to my aid. Stubie, heavy-chested, did the same.

Mike's voice quavered as he answered my question: "The history of the world." Really his Oral topic?

"*The history of the*...You sure?" I jolted.

He nodded gravely.

I tried humouring him. The others tittered, including Robin. "I want to talk about war...," Mike grated, and yes, he crimsoned.

"Not about food, pastries?".

Yves looked at me crossly; he figured I underestimated Mike, underestimated them all.

"A short history of the world it'll be," Mike said, lips tightening.

Unconsciously I began taking Mike seriously: I imagined him reading about the history of food, and what people in far corners of the world consumed (and some who didn't because of scarcity and poverty).

Yves appeared distraught, something grinding in him—like what occurred only in a bird's stomach. *Yeah!*

        .   ***

Again for the Oral assignment I encouraged them to talk about topical social issues, if they so wished, what's written about in the op-ed columns in the daily newspapers or discussed on the radio and TV by talk-show types, if they didn't want to talk about career choices in pastry-making.

Strange: no-one wanted to talk about pastry-making—nothing about cooking or baking, like it was beneath them. My colleagues' faces stiffened when I told them about my students' new interests. I was having a strange effect on my charges, and because they thought about where I came from...and, what I could possibly learn from them?

Stubie didn't guffaw anymore. "The history of the world," Mike intoned. Yves kept to himself, though he again muttered something to Mike, sotto voce. *Giving him advice?*

Where would Mike get his research ideas and information from? I tried imagining him spending hours in the college library poring over peer-reviewed journals; but he wasn't the type. *History of the World*...I yet humoured him.

"The Encyclopaedia, Internet..." Mike moaned back to me.

Caril grew contemplative. Stubie next to her sniffed like a bloodhound. He pawed her arm, then nibbled her sleeves.

Mike walked away from them...and from me, intent on his Oral. His final essay topic would be "A Short History of the World"– I must know. I mustn't underestimate him; not underestimate any of them. Christ, tell my teaching colleagues!

On Yves' mind Quebec's future weighed heavily, I contemplated.

Meeka huddled with the others, and again talked about going out west to be with her beau after graduation, like going to a new country. A new Canada in the making. *Really, Meeka?*

Would the west separate from Canada? *Now everyone wanted to go out west.* Oh, Robin to get married.

"Gosh, you're so skinny," someone shot at Robin. "You'd end up at the Montreaux Clinic in Vancouver!"

"Na," snarled Robin.

"You want to be as skinny as Princess Di then?"

"I wish."

Meeka's girlfriend with two kids, the party-girl, would she also go out west? Stubie burst out laughing. Caril looked at me, frowning.

Mike appeared irritable-looking. *A Short History of the World* was taking its toll on him. *Incredible!* My charges of a generation ago amidst trade winds blowing...and canefields bristling. Sugar and molasses in my veins, what seemed now, well, strange or unpredictable. *Yes, let them eat cake!* I tried to imagine these Caterers going on to use only genuine Demerara sugar—like where I was born.

The Caribbean being my own place. *Whither Castro?*

***

Again I imagined my colleagues scoffing, or laughing. My teaching days were numbered, I vaguely thought about. Time being the great leveller, and history never being real, but only part of the grand illusion. Plato's Cave, you see.

Time for the Orals to begin, like the high point of my teaching career. Caril, in her typical manner, was confident, but she day-dreamed a lot. She chuckled. Stubie pretended he was busier than he actually was; he seemed nervous. Meeka was fazed-looking. I was prepared to listen to their talks with appreciation, indeed. *Now who wanted to speak first?*

Yves's hand shot up.

"Why...*first?*" I asked him, becoming intrigued.

He shrugged, "To get it over an' done with."

I wondered about his commitment to French separatism, if not to French classical literature. Mike, still in his own space with his "History of the World" in the making. Everyone's body posture was rigid; body language was all. The Orals were starting to take their toll.

Yves took his stance in front of the class; he began talking about Canada's largest province—as he called it—and about the durable "French fact" He wanted to impress, if not surprise, me maybe. He quoted Pierre Vallieres' *White Who...of America?*

Everyone looked at him admonishingly, because they detected my own self-awareness, if just an intimation of my sense of living in a new country. Yves settled down to it, as he talked earnestly about "Good Health," make no mistake about—the Virtues of Good Health.

Stubie tittered. The others listened, well, keenly.

Yves, handsome-looking, grew in his stride. One day he'd be the best damned pastry maker around! Not a classical scholar anymore, yeah. Stubie would speak next–he also wanting to get it over and done with. Meeka, Robin, Doug, Caril, and the others to follow. Mike would speak last—if only to prolong his anxiety. Really about the history of the world?

Yves kept being at it, taking a longer time. He announced to the class the three main ways, or *virtues*...to maintain good health. *First*, eat a balanced diet.

Yeah-yeah!

Yves paused, scratching his dishevelled head of hair. Meeka and her group tittered. Caril smiled in her individual way. Stubie grinned–he was known to be an *eater*. He'd said jokingly "I could eat a baby...," when he was really hungry! "Sure you would, like a cannibal," Caril snapped back at him. "I eat only sitting down; cannibals eat standing up," Stubie retorted, quoting an Ethiopian proverb.

Yves continued about the *second* thing...to do for good health, indeed for one to exercise regularly. Again everyone nodded.

Yeah-yeah.

Meeka boasted about soon going on a rigorous exercise program in Calgary in order to please her beau. She didn't want to be a fat bride! Chuffed laughter. Sure, I also laughed. Caril made a face.

Yves didn't like the interruption, he was impatient. The *third* reason for good health...? He whirred. Everyone figured he'd say something... like try to get a good sleep; or...avoid stress! Stubie let out with impatience, "Yeah, what's the third reason, bud?

"Tell us!" barked another. *Separatism?*

Yves had a captive audience. The politician in him, a French-Canadian fact, Quiet Revolution and all. The new Canada in the making, Instinctively I whirred. Mike lifted his neck, crane-like, in eager anticipation.

Yves looked at his audience disdainfully.

Harold, with a serious mien—who never said much— yelled, "Come on, Yves, you don't have all day, what's the third reason?"

Yves lifted his head, almost like a scorpion about to strike. Imperious, yes. Meeka let out an involuntary sound, a whistle blowing. Thinking about Calgary, she was. Her friend with two kids, what did she look like? Did Meeka really want to fix me up because I seemed to be a loner? *Not an outsider?*

"The *third* reason for good health," tempted Yves, "is..."

"Yeah– "

"*Smoke dope,*" said Yves, seriously.

Caril burst out laughing. Stubie made a hissing sound. Yvonne and Brian did the same. Yves meant what he said, as he grimaced; and he remained stone-silent, taking in his audience.

More laughter. And I was bound to ask: *Why smoke dope?*

"Why...Yves?" everyone chorussed. Yves focussed his gaze on each one of them. "You smoke dope, well...to be in a good humour; it's important for good health." He smiled gleefully, determined to have the last laugh.

The joke was on us, see. On me most of all, ah. And Yves was in no mood to be challenged, like a genuine French fact.

***

The other students took their turn in front of the class and they talked about one social topic or another—mostly about issues relating to suicide, euthanasia, abortion. Caril was eloquent about protecting the environment, an "ecology freak" she called herself. Meeka discussed the pros and cons of abortion. No one wanted to talk about what it meant to be a good caterer!

Mike raised his neck, looming large, he wasn't to be ignored. The "History of the World" still in the making, as he stood in front of the class. But he was shy, even nervous; his physical presence, gangly and all, teeth jutting out. He was no mere pastry-maker I must know.

He droned on, reading from his prepared text, a jumble of notes he'd collected. His voice barely audible; but he was determined to read everything he'd copied down about the First and Second World Wars. Dates, facts, and Winston Churchill's name being dropped at random. After a long fifteen minutes, I sensed that only Yves listened to him, intently.

My patience was running out with Mike; but he kept on talking, for almost an hour. *That... long?* Caril looked at me. Stubie stifled a guffaw. Caril nudged him hard in the rib. "Ouch," Stubie let out, the fart. Mike wiped perspiration from his face and neck.

Applause came from everyone...in the end. Polite, but impatient, you see. And about what was really educational, if not inspirational, and what wasn't. Places near or far coming closer in my mind's eye. Odd, I figured Mike and Yves would now become friends: one English, the other French. The solitudes no longer seemed real in Canada...or elsewhere—where I may have come from—if because of my special way of teaching.

Trade winds blowing; and I imagined my colleagues' faces after being told about the history of the world. *Go on, tell them more.*

Outside the classroom a few students huddled together, chatting, and laughing their hearts out. Mike's eyes lit up among them. Yes, the real history of the world. Caril looked at me again, if forlornly. Meeka sneered. No longer going out west to the real heartland, was she?

One of my teaching colleagues approached, then made a sudden about turn. Meeka simply said she was relieved that the "Orals" were over, done with— like a new phase in her life. Once more she sat next to me cheek by jowl and muttered about another party her friend was having—the friend with two kids. It'd be a farewell party...before she too went out west.

But this time Meeka didn't invite me; for she knew I wouldn't come. Yves and Mike kept talking to each other; as Yves grew strangely tall...taller than Mike.

Meeka nudged me. She suddenly wanted me to be at the party; oh, she had guile. And Winnipeg, Calgary, Vancouver...kept calling. Caril murmured something about why start a new life. *What for, Meeka?*

"I'm getting married, Caril-dear," cackled Meeka. "Not you... to Stubie? Has he proposed yet?"

Stubie laughed, then flexed his biceps. Robin came and playfully cuffed Meeka. Mike hummed something or the other, as Yves listened intently. Canada's, if not Quebec's future really weighed on them all. Mike insisted on place-names, like Dieppe and Normandy. Yves smiled–the sweetest smile I ever saw. I figured he would truly attend an Ivy League school, if not in the USA, then in France...if he didn't make it as a caterer in Canada.

I said to Meeka that I would attend her party; but she knew I wouldn't.

I regretted the term coming to an end as my colleagues kept asking if I'd been too easy on them–the students they meant— and looked at me with a strange awe, because I may have figured out my own place in Canada, yes.

THE GUITAR

Night: and the house rumbled and shook as another truck lumbered past not far from the Voyageur Colonial Bus Terminal on Lyon Street; the house was an anachronism among adjacent ones forming a row, almost like a block of slum dwellings. The bare walls of my room were mouldy, plaster cracking. Closing my eyes, I wondered why I'd decided to come here where the first "Room for Rent" sign caught my eye. A musty smell floated up in the semi-darkness. An occasional cough and moan, then guitar strains, funereal-sounding; and the sensation of having travelled to be here...was still with me.

Morning light filtered in, and I rubbed my eyes. I was finally glad to be here. But peeled plaster on the walls kept coming at me. Slowly, I opened the door...without expectancy. Suddenly from the opposite room, the door flung open, and a voice jabbered at me. Polish-sounding, or some other European tongue. Then the door slammed shut, and *he* disappeared inside. Last night's whimpers, moans...guitar-strains again. *Yeah, welcome.*

In Ottawa: the Prime Minister's residence on Sussex Drive and the Parliament Buildings where they passed the Immigration Laws. Gingerly I walked down the stairs, my heart in my mouth. A crackle, then laughter. An older man with a paunch moved about in the kitchen, beaming when he saw me; and he wanted company. "Ah, laddie," he sang, extending a trunk-like arm, "you're new here. Jake's the name."

In his late seventies he was...quite unlike the one upstairs in the room opposite mine. "Did you hear the guitarist last night?" Jake asked. I shook my head. Jake twisted his lips and pointed to the attic. I asked about the Pole, whoever he was, upstairs.

"Take no notice o' him. Harmless as a butterfly, he is." Jake laughed, body convulsing. "I've been around here long enough to know." He wheezed hard. "Being born in Ottawa an' all I am," and he stabbed a finger at me. "Where d'you come from, eh?"

Come from? Not waiting for an answer, Jake went on about "them days". The Depression, see...not so long ago, I've slept in worse places." He'd travelled across Canada, I must know, criss-crossing to Edmonton, Calgary, then again to St. John's, Sydney, Halifax. His Depression train kept going. In Thunder Bay he'd stared up at the Sleeping Giant, Nanabijou, and looked across at the Native reservation close to Mount McKay. "Yeah, Indians they're, some lazy, ah; but I don't blame them."

Jake didn't believe his own words, what he kept telling me, as he furrowed his brows. "Lake Superior's also in me, I kept going across Canada." He took me next to Whitehorse and Alaska, then along the TransCanada Highway and back to Winnipeg, Saskatoon, as I kept going with him. Jake ambled around the kitchen; and he was also in a huge wilderness park in northern Ontario where he lived in bush camps and planted trees. *I must know!*

He lowered his voice, as if he didn't want to be heard.

Yeah, he'd fallen into muskegs, and millions of blackflies, mosquitoes, attacked him. "It's true, mark my words, lad." *How true?* Guitar strains coming from the attic I rehearsed in my mind. Jake moaned hard.

"I'll die in this city, not in Toronto, eh?" He made a gargoyle's face. "Yeah, in Toronto, there where you'll find people packed like sardine in a can. See them in the subway, tramcar, everywhere on Yonge Street, Spadina, Jarvis." Jake bulged with a strange laugh. The one upstairs...the Pole... would he come down now?

I was on tenterhooks, sort of. "Lad, when they put me in the ground I'll still fight to get out kicking an' screaming," Jake laughed. My turn to laugh. Then back to the Depression days, like what he kept making up: "In Sudbury I was a bartender, a barber, doing every job you could think of." He breathed in hard, and he grew florid.

He started coughing convulsively. I handed him a glass of water, and he gulped it. "Lad, I'm ready to meet my Maker, Catholic as I am. But I'll not make it easy for Him yet." His fleshy mouth creased with a smile. He made a sign of the cross. Then, "Have you met him?"

"Who?"

"The one upstairs, playing that...*thing?* He came in yesterday morning, and not a word he said. Played all night long; it's driving the other one upstairs crazy too, yeah." *The Pole?* Jake dipped into his milky-white soup, a bulbous drip forming on his nose. Fate brought me here, I thought.

Jake eyed me warily. "You know what that does to an old man's nerves?" He banged a spoon against the table.

Ah, someone was coming down the stairs, and Jake stood rigid. I gripped the window sill overlooking the street. The Pole entered; a tallish man, bedraggled-looking, his face a distinct stubble, like a thousand ants crawling over his chin and neck. I was getting a good look at him. He didn't make eye contact with me. He sat down at the kitchen table, then quickly got up and hurried back up the stairs.

"You've got to trust some people sometime," Jake growled.

I apprehensively kept looking up the stairs. The Depression train stopped moving; the window almost shuttered. But light crept in. Jake eyed me. *Will you?*

—Will I what?

***

45

I heard him leaving the room in the attic, and now coming down; yes, I'd kept following his guitar strains. Skinny he was, and pimpled at the ridge of his nose. He was dressed in faded blue jeans. He eyed me, and frowned. "Nice guitar-playing you have," I lied, Jake's mood had infected me.

Earl, he said his name was. He shook his head.

"You been playing long?" I asked.

Cornflakes disappeared before his nostrils as he ate. "I just got outa prison," he said. The guitar's strains a wail. "I did time, for..."

What? "We all have to, sooner or later," he grated. Instinctively I looked away from him. "I was in for stealing, man." Cornflakes smeared his chin.

Earl's footsteps throbbed as he went back up the stairs to the attic.

You've got to trust some people sometime: Jake's words; the Depression train still rolling across Canada. *Why am I here?* I would get accustomed to the rooming house. Not ever the Prime Minister's residence on Sussex Drive?

I looked through the scarred window to the bus terminal across the street. Vehicles going and coming. Maybe a transient of sorts I was. But not like Earl, the guitar-player...or, the Pole in the room opposite mine? Coughs, loud wheezes.

Jake said to me: "So you've finally met him?"

I told him about Earl being in prison. "It figures, that type," Jake concluded. "During the Depression it was bad, but there were always honest people around. It's a shame, he's so young. Stay clear of him. He'll come to no good, lad." Yeah, Jake called me that...*lad*.

Police coming to the house that night, banging against the doors. *Looking for Earl?* "Leave him alone," I cried to the police, but voiceless. The Pole tramping down the stairs, crying "Murder!" A nightmare I was having. More trucks lumbered by. The landlord said the Pole had threatened to jump off the Empire State Building in New York.

The police shaking their heads.

You've got to trust...some people. Jake's words again. "Don't mind me, lad; but see, the guitar's really driving me crazy," he whined. Odd, the guitar began to sound familiar to me now.

From the top of the stairs Jake called out, "Keep an old man company, lad. Don't leave, I mean." *Leave?*

—Yeah, me.

***

Two weeks passed quickly. I bided my time, listening, remembering...talking to myself. Jake, where was he now? A knock on my door, and Earl shoved his guitar before me. "Want to buy it?" The guitar was greyish-white with distinctive studs and sequins, like diamond beads pimpling the sides; embroidered-looking.

It came from Las Vegas and might have once been owned by Chet Atkins. *Said who?* "Go on, take it," Earl insisted.

"I don't..."

"Don't what?"

"I don't know how to play."

"You'll soon learn."

"I..."

"You've been listening to me, I know. And him upstairs." He meant Jake; his eyes crinkled. The guitar's design, and signs, symbols, on the well-formed handle.

"I've found a job," Earl said. "I need money to buy lunch, man." He shifted uncomfortably; made a snarly face. Ottawa: should I leave here? I kept looking at the guitar.

"Give me ten bucks, and it's yours," Earl snapped.

I imagined strumming, being a Spanish classical guitarist. My playacting, yeah. Earl was almost threatening, see. "You really found a job?" I asked, tentative. "You really need the money to buy lunch?" Like a plea in my voice.

A rakish grin crept across Earl's angular face.

"I'll give you ten dollars. Repay me when you can, and I'll return the guitar," I said.

"You can have the guitar for keeps."

Oh?

My fingers on the strings, I strummed tentatively. Jake, well, he would get used to my playing. Earl pocketed my ten dollars and hurried back up the attic. Depression trains criss-crossing Canada as Jake wheezed upstairs. The Pole...where was he?

Jake hobbled back down the stairs; he'd overheard us. "It could be hot stuff, lad," he said.

"You told me to trust...didn't you?"

Jake made a sick face.

"He's found a job. He needs money to buy food."

"I know," murmured Jake.

You know?

Jake told me about stolen food from the pantry. Then, "Before long you too will be a musician, eh? Making an ol' man's life miserable," and he moaned lugubriously. The Depression train again, as I played at strumming; played at being, well, a member of the *Guess Who*? I was a real Canadian. My being Gordon Lightfoot too, you bet.

Earl was now working, and hunger no longer gnawed at his insides. I imagined playing at a huge concert, like Woodstock. Not being a classical guitarist any longer? Jake hummed to me, "Play as long as you like; I'm just an old man, I'll die soon."

"You will not, Jake."

"I will, lad."

I hugged the guitar to my chest. *Oh, trust some people.* Caribbean waves started coming from a far shore as I "played," well, longer. The Pole talked to himself, guttural-sounding...in his room.

Jake hummed, "It's the way life is. He...leaving, just like that, it's too bad." *Earl...left?* The guitar was really mine now.

Jake again talked about dying. And yes, about the Pole... jumping off the Empire State Building. Not from the Parliament Buildings, or from the Prime Minister's Residence on Sussex Drive? *Where really?*

***

Earl's room would soon be rented, as the landlord snapped his fingers. Oh, people coming and going at the bus terminal. Outsiders all, but like whom I didn't want to be. Jake's Depression train once more. "Too many foreigners come here; the politicians should do something about it," Jake talking to himself. Soliloquy, not colloquy.

I began thinking of returning the guitar to Earl. But the instrument's fancy beads and embroidered patterns kept me to it. I started taking guitar lessons at the local YMCA. Ottawa: here I come!

"You will soon become a professional," Jake wheezed again. I laughed, and he laughed back at me.

And the lessons at the "Y" on Argyle Street on Saturday mornings became all. I began playing "*Friar Jacques...*" without rhythm or style. The other students laughed at my pretended strumming. I laughed at myself, too.

Back at the rooming house Jake looked sallow, almost yellow; he was seeing his doctor again. The rooming house once more shook. In my room the paint peeled, strips hanging. The Pole glared at me at the top of the stairs. With the guitar in hand, I blinked.

The "Y" began to be like a regular place for hangers-on, drop-outs.

A scruffy-looking youth I observed lying on a sofa in the lounge; and Jake's Depression days were yet with me. *Trust some people....* It was Earl on the sofa, his thin mouth a distinct leer.

He didn't recognize me. "Want to buy this?" He flashed a gold ring at me. "Eh?" I hissed. *Not working?*

"Remember me, Earl?" I tried.

"Shit, never set eyes on you before." He pulled back the ring. "I need cash to buy food!" Then, "I found a job, man." Again he shoved the ring at me.

"What about the ten bucks you owe me?" He still didn't recognize me. "It's your guitar, not mine, Earl," I parlayed.

"I don't know you, shit!" His lanky frame stretched out. The ring before me, solid gold. "You want it, yes or no? Earl arched himself over me. The guitar's strumming in the attic. The Depression train moving. Earl yawned...vacantly; he really did.

Jake didn't laugh when I told him about meeting Earl...and the ring, like a solid offering. The guitar in my hand, a string broken; it fell down, and another string snapped. Jake wheezed; and more yellowish he looked, jaundiced. I kept wanting to be a classical guitarist and travelling to Barcelona in Spain, then to Guadalajara, Mexico. Not being Johnny Cash on the Depression train anymore!

At the "Y" the front desk clerk, a blonde woman with an attractive smile, marvelled at me playing the guitar. I fantasized being Bob Dylan. "You could be good at it, you belong to San Francisco. You're the type," Maylene said.

The rhythm of lasting love: ah, somewhere. I was no newcomer. "The *type*?" I replied.

Maylene flitted her eyelashes. Jake yet with me...to Saskatoon...or the Lakehead. A train's noise, whistle blowing. Jake's Lake Superior, see. Northern Ontario and prairie winds kept blowing.

A twosome: one heavyset, bearded; the other thin, sensitive-looking, an artist. *Do I know them?* Maylene smiled at me. "Know what?" she said, like an invitation. A sing-along at the "Y' was being planned, a benefit for old folks, and the disabled. *True?*

The twosome were musicians from the Maritimes. Maylene said they genuinely wanted to help people. I heard Jake wheeze louder. *I was heading somewhere now.* "It'd be great if we had. an extra guitar. Forgot mine in Newfoundland," said Bob, the bearded one.

"We'd been planning on not going back fishing. But..." hummed the skinny one.

But?

Earl, what was he up to now? Maylene repeated the word *fishing,* and smiled. Mickey, the skinny one, had come to Ottawa to do some good, he said. "I guess you'll have to buy a guitar from somewhere, Bob," he said in a baleful tone. *Not steal one?*

"I have a guitar..." I muttered.

"You do?"

"Sure."

Trust some people. "How much, well...d'you want for it?" Bob threw at me. Mickey put on his dark glasses. The guitar was worth about fifty dollars, not ten...decorative studs an' all. Earl's Las Vegas instrument, see. "I could *lend* it to you," I said.

Mickey beamed. Bob gleamed, also. Maylene once more flitted her eyes—what I carried all the way home with me. The Pole in his room whimpered. His memory…fading, if now forbidding. I twisted my lips, like my own pain. Earl, where was he?

***

The phone rang. Bob: *How would you like to sell the guitar?* Earl's…hot stuff. The police coming to the rooming house, yes. "Murder!" voices called out. The sing-along cheered me on. That ring Earl was trying to pass off on me.

"Yeah, I will eventually sell it," I said to Bob…about the guitar.

Laughter at the other end of the line, Maylene's.

The twosome came to my door on Cooper Street. They examined the guitar's ornamental studs. I merely dwelled on a rousing sing-a-long with these two being featured performers… making others less fortunate happy. *Really happy.*

"How much d'you want for it?" Mickey asked.

"Ten bucks."

Bob fished into his pocket. Mickey gloated with a smile. And Earl indeed working, I thought; and that ring; and the rooming house shaking as another truck lumbered past. The paint, the walls, coming undone. And my now living on Sussex Drive at the Prime Minister's Residence. On Parliament Hill politicians debating a new bill about an Immigration Green Paper. Not one about Native people's rights?

I looked at the guitar, then handed it to Bob—he with his empty pocket an' all. *'Friar Jacques…?'* Bob wrote an IOU note. *Ten dollars.*

He shook my hand. "It's nice doing business with you." Mickey said, and laughed. Maylene still smiling, yeah.

I, Jake being carted off in an ambulance and crying out: "You've got to trust some people, lad!"

Famous last words… the guitar's strains in the air.

Maylene was no longer smiling. "There's no sing-a-long," she said. She looked prettier than ever, lipsticked mouth an' all.

"Why not?" I asked.

"Those two guys, they skipped town."

Earl came towards me, demanding his guitar back…from me? He pulled out a new ring from his middle finger, like a magical trick.

Maylene laughed. "Ten bucks only, see," Earl said, offering the ring.

Old Man Jake…somewhere waving, calling me *laddie*. Not just a newcomer! The train chug-chugging along, hooting loudly. And the Pole might have disappeared for good. At the terminal I imagined buses coming and going more than usual…or departing, if disappearing, all across Canada. *Believe me*.

THE HOUSE

"As a colonial...remove yourself from what you know, and become blest personally."

—**V.S. Naipaul**

B landishment spreads across his face as he talks about how he'd lived in London and worked at the Savoy Hotel. "It's the largest hotel anywhere," Roy boasted, eyes gleaming. Indeed it's about his desire to own a house after leaving Mauritius. London keeps coming closer: Piccadilly Circus, Hyde Park, Trafalgar Square. *But we're in Canada.* "Man, in London the price of everything shot up! I couldn't save enough to buy that house. My salary at the Savoy wasn't big enough."

Roy scolds all of Britain and the English race for his lost opportunity. "What better place it'd be to own a house than London?" he throws at me; as Mauritius sinks deeper into the Indian Ocean. "If I worked hard, save everything I'd soon own

53

that house." He wrinkles his flat forehead. "I did everything in my power, worked two jobs, night and day shifts. If I made it in London it'd be a dream come true." He twirls his long, thin fingers. "Nothing beats owning a house," he declares, denying his anonymity.

My own desire to travel across Canada as a new immigrant with me. *How...new?* I will start with St. John's on the far east coast and eventually end up in Whitehorse in the Northwest. I will visit where the Vikings had settled in Newfoundland centuries ago, then go to where John Cabot's *Mathew* had landed.

Roy keeps me glued to London. "As long as I had enough for the down payment I'd own this house," he says, sucking in air. "I thought of ways of decorating that house, have the best furniture ornate style, and the best material, granite, light fixtures." He's unstoppable. "Panelling, carpeting, posh marble floor; then I'd invite friends to come and visit me—to really see me in London!" *Friends he left behind in Mauritius?*

I imagine coming from Mauritius, too. "No, no," Roy flutters his hands. Then, "I met many interesting people at the Savoy, dignitaries, you see." Like a revelation, you bet.

"Dignitaries," I echo.

Roy disdains the word "immigrants," as he makes a clucking sound. And his friends would include the rich and famous: Prince Charles, and other royalty all with him in his dream-house...where he imagines sipping tea and eating scones with his friends in elegant English style. *Dream on!* Roy, who's come from a strict Hindu family, his father in Mauritius, a devotee—a hibiscus garland around his neck as he does his morning prayers; and words hummed from the Bhagavada Gita with young Roy dutifully sitting next to his father. *Ohmmm!*

"How could I afford it?" Roy rails, "you tell me!"

"Tell you?'"

"The house!" Then, "It's not right!" He thumps his chest, almost dramatic.

Roy forlornly walking around London on wet foggy days and nights aiming for his dream house. But he's now here, in Canada, in biting cold weather. "Everywhere I went I'd tried mixing with

English people, men and women in the pubs. I even attended special night-shows."

I am enthralled.

"I was like a lost soul in the capital of the world," he mourns. *Do I want to hear more?* "Then one day," Roy adds, like his moment of epiphany, "I came upon a couple talking about Canada. It was God's blessing, see." I inhale hard.

Roy looks at me in his moment tinged with excitement. "Canada, a great wilderness country with lakes everywhere... and abundant fish and game," *God's country?* Roy read this in a tourist brochure, and imagined himself in khaki with rifle in hand going on a jungle safari. No African landscape for him.

"My house, it'd be more than an igloo," Roy hums to me, like a forewarning. Oh, the joke's on me...with my own self-realization. Tell him I want to travel across Canada; I'm really a *Canadian.*

"This couple, you see...they were indeed Canadians," Roy goes on. "I started making plans immediately."

But a wan look spreads across his dark face, at how I'm taking him. *He...taking me?* "I came across the *Plain Truth* magazine"; and he'd started listening to *The World Tomorrow,* Herbert W Armstrong, the Christian evangelist, on the radio and TV. *His Hindu father... still garlanded?*

Roy reveals that *evil* prevented him from owning his dream-house. He laments seeing young people dressed in saffron robes, heads shaven, who handed out leaflets at the Victoria station in London and chanted mantras. *Hare Krishna hippies?* He breathes in hard.

"I figured..."

"What?"

"I must experience a new life."

Our unplanned meeting at the "Y" here in Ottawa, like our destined meeting place. Indeed here not far from where the Rideau and Ottawa rivers meet, and where early pioneers like Jacques Cartier and Champlain had long ago come to build a new country.

Roy taps me on the shoulder, "I found work easily at the Savoy in London, remember." *Yes, Canada, you see.* "But here the only job

I could get is being a dishwasher." He looks around warily. "I sat in the park across Elgin Street and watched old men in shabby clothes, then it's government workers in designer clothes walking by....and where was I?" Remorse mixed with anger in his voice.

"Again I started thinking of that house," he continues.

Nothing about Christian evangelism? The Lord Elgin Hotel not far away; and had there been a ship with that name that took indentured immigrants from the Indian subcontinent to places like Mauritius and Guyana? Unconsciously I think about my forebears—with history in the mix.

He continues, "I don't just want to wash dishes in a restaurant." Pause. "Ah, how could I own a house if I only do menial work?" Did I not want to help him achieve his dream?

Now...where must we go?

"I must have a skill," he says, gripping my sleeves. "It says so in the *Plain Truth*—like a prophecy about to come true." *Oh?* "I'm bilingual, I have talent," he lets out.

"Yes, talent."

"Bilingual as we all are in Mauritius." It's his declaration of being no longer with the English in London. Then he reveals that he'd found a job at the Rideau Club often visited by members of Parliament. "They were impressed...that I'd worked at the Savoy in London."

The Rideau Club where he'd also met Princess Diana? "I'm still there at the Rideau Club, but working as a cleaner."

He drops his hands and starts walking away. I tighten my own lips. Awe and pity everywhere.

***

Roy's voice with me, in my growing immigrant self-awareness, and two weeks quickly go by. Then a month. When we meet he talks once more about the house. And, you see, he indeed wants to acquire a new skill. His cheekbones rise...he'd quit his job at the Rideau Club. His youthful days with garlands festooned around his neck? *His father's eyes closed in a long Hindu prayer.*

"I must have a real skill," Roy pokes at me. "That house, man!"

I nod, indulgently.

He declares that he has a natural talent for barbering.

"Barbering?" He, with his fifties crewcut!

But the joke on me, I figure, like a game or prank we're playing on each other. Another week quickly goes by; and have I seen the last of Roy?

The next Sunday morning there's a knock at the front door of my Cooper Street apartment building. I shuffle down the flight of stairs of the white-stoned building expecting to be greeted by a Seventh Day Adventist caller. Roy doesn't apologize for coming at six in the morning.

"Look, I must practise on your head," he declares.

"What?"

"I have a natural talent for barbering." He whips out a pair of scissors. Then, "Trust me!"

"Trust you?"

In my apartment, he snips at my hair. I dodge left and right. He thrusts the scissors around, moving my head in a different position each time, like a professional. "You must trust me!"

I lean forward, becoming submissive. Roy beams, "I have to do a test tomorrow, I'm taking a course."

"You are?"

Snippets of hair fall left and right. Sure, I needed a haircut. Roy's face suffused as he pulls strands of hair at the back, then at the top of my head. He's been taking lessons at *Ann Dixie's*: he already paid the four hundred and fifty dollars fee. *Snip! Snip!*

He stands back, admiring his handiwork. The course is scheduled for twelve weeks, and he has attended classes twice.

"Are you serious?"

"Ah," he cries.

I firmly hold his hand. It'll be his new *profession*, I must know.

"How many are in your class, Roy?"

"Fourteen." He snips faster.

"Any other male?"

"I'm the only one."

"You...with thirteen girls? You lucky devil," I tease.

57

"Thirteen's an unlucky number," he pulls back; but his hands are electrically charged as he snips away. "You're getting a good cut, man." Then, "I'm looking forward to my class tonight."

"Any particular reason?"

"They think I am clumsy." Pause. "But look at what a good job I'm doing with your hair." He forces my head into the mirror. "I'm really going to show them...tonight."

My thoughts drift back to that house—maybe a smallish place downtown in the upper-end Sandy Hill neighbourhood. Customers flocking...to be at the latest hot-shot hair-designer salon. *Yves St Laurent he keeps being, and visited by clients from the embassies, and from executive government types. Politicians and other hot-shots all want to have the best cut.* Bilingual in Canada he is, note well.

Savoy Hotel days in London...no longer. Ads placed in the newspapers, magazines, TV, Internet. The Prime Minister of Canada inviting him to his Sussex Drive residence to have a special cut. A magazine article emblazons with the lead:

"NEW IMMIGRANT SUCCESS STORY."

Roy's picture adorns magazine covers. He smiles beatifically. His distant father in Mauritius is still adenoidal with *ohms*. I keep thinking about my own immigrant self, like tragic relief. *Travelling across Canada—am I?*

* * *

I am with my own immigrant excitement. Roy...he is without the usual blandishment at *Ann Dixie's,* the girls or women around him with coy looks; they closely watch how his fingers twirl, hands moving with electrical compulsion—almost with amusement. He tells them about wanting to own a dream house?

My own hair I look at in the mirror, the edges ragged. I begin feeling anxious...about my own state in Canada. Immigrant angst, more perplexing. My not coming from India, or the Caribbean, like my veritable place. I begin heading for Banff on the west coast of Canada, then over the Rockies; I no longer want to be an *outsider.*

Sunday night I walk into the YMCA, like my special haunt. Roy is there, looking suspicious. Glued to the wide TV screen with five or six others, all watching the *Miss World* beauty pageant. Women in swim-wear, then in elegant evening gowns— representatives of Ecuador, U.S., Britain, India, Russia, Sweden, *you name it.*

"Where were you?" I whisper to him.

"I quit, man."

"What...where?"

"Ann Dixie's."

The TV screen's contestants answer questions about their ambition; the contest is being held in London at the Savoy, oh.

"What for?"

"They gave me a girl's head to practice on...a dummy."

"What's wrong with that?"

The others in the TV room turn and look at us.

"I had to put on curlers; I was supposed to take half an hour." Roy sucks in air. *A contestant from the Far East is now on, the TV cameras rolling. A beauty from Mauritius...speaking in French. An interpreter with an English accent interprets with a smile.*

"I took the entire day," Roy's voice a suppressed squeal.

The next beauty contestant is from Canada, who chuckles as she answers questions about her belief in God. Her hair elegantly coiffed. The finalists will soon be announced.

I want the Canadian among the finalists, my heart beating faster. "Ann Dixie said not to return," Roy moans.

The Caribbean's steamy streets: this one particular contestant flaunting her Afro-hairstyle. Suddenly I don't like being in Canadian winter. The TV announcer hints at who the winner will be. Yes, the Caribbean beauty with a distinct lilt in her voice rises above the others at the Savoy Hotel. *London calling!*

I persist travelling across Canada, a pioneer of sorts, believe me. Wheat fields gleam in the sun. The Canadian contestant once more on the screen speaking in French.

The winner is...

"Oh Canada," the anthem being played; everyone in the room with us are all alive. I rub my eyes, and I expect Roy to do the same. Trade winds blowing with the familiar smell of mollusc, seaweed, somewhere in the Caribbean Sea. Not the Indian Ocean with Mauritius in the background.

Roy gets up, he glares at me. "I don't have much time to waste, man!" *His father still muttering ohms.* Pulling my bluff Roy hurls, "I'm going to Montreal, I am bilingual. We all are in Mauritius, yes."

The new beauty queen is being crowned and everyone in the room cheers. "It's not like you people who say you're Canadian but are not. Yes—not bilingual," Roy throws at me, "who only speak English, and..."

I wait.

"Rubbish!"

Roy putting on curlers on the dummy head at Ann Dixie's. Thirteen women huddling round him.

The real runners-up at the beauty contest are from ...Jamaica, the UK, USA, India. The crowned queen enthusiastically waves a maple leaf Canadian flag.

Yeah, incredible!

***

Roy, dapper-looking in a business suit and almost unrecognizable hurries down Wellington Street not far from the Parliament Buildings. Earlier that day a Lebanese had hijacked a bus in Montreal and he came to Ottawa threatening to blow up the Parliament Buildings if his family members back in war-torn Beirut aren't allowed to come to Canada as refugees.

Police cars, media types, are everywhere! Cameras on tripods, and lights flashing. It's the big news story. One report blares out that the Lebanese immigrant is a religious nut. *What else?*

Roy's hair combed straight back, slick-looking; I watch him quickly moving away like he's running away from me and everyone else. "Roy," I call out. A cold northern wind slaps at my face.

"I must go, man," he hollers back.

"Go...where?"

"That house...*la maison*, remember?"

The media crowing about the Lebanese being a religious nut. Odd, again I think about the beauty contest on TV, and the winner...with Roy walking arm-in-arm. A stronger wind blows, as I run my fingers through my hair. Cold winter a-coming. But it's to Montreal, the "City of Saints," like being nowhere else, ah.

I shift my gaze back to the Peace Tower on Parliament Hill, and also looking down the street hoping to see Roy turn around... and to wave...to the Lebanese man. *Not...to me only*? Our life's beginning...without an ending.

PART TWO

MUSKEG

L arry champions his own name being an Ojibwa—now like my real introduction to Northern Ontario. Tall, rough-hewn in his style and manner he is. Yes, Canada—a special place with Lester Pearson, Pierre Trudeau, I know... and EXPO-67 in Montreal. On campus I watched Jane Fonda lambaste the US of A over the B-52 bombers raging over Vietnam. The Berrigan brothers, and Noam Chomsky. The Beatles' "Eleanor Rigby" also with me. And my being here in a wilderness of sorts among long-haired students strumming guitars, each a Neil Young, and mimicking Joni Mitchell.

But Larry insists that I contemplate the Great Spirit only. Nanabijou, the Sleeping Giant, at the Lakehead. "Ahh," he calls out, "you think you're the only real Indian, eh?"

We plant more trees, work I seem fated to do. Yeah, back-breaking work that must be done. I will be a true Canadian. *How... true?* Echoes: a grandmother in the tropics, and my mother, also.

Spruce, pine and other seedlings in the bag on my shoulder, my being indeed here in Northern Ontario. Yes, the trees we put into the ground. Larry glances over at me.

I scuff the topsoil hard once more. He keeps watching me, Larry does. Mother-Earth, he calls it. Moss, grass, logs with charcoal before us after the forest fire. He shows me how to really plant the trees. We move uphill, then downhill, over more burnt-out areas. *Mother-fucker!* he cries.

Larry smirks knowing that the crew bosses, the Lakehead University forestry farts, are lording it over us. A woodpecker rat-tats away. Three other Cree planters join us; and sweaty, tired I am. Blackflies and mosquitoes take off chunks of soggy sandwich from my hand, ah. "This forest's ours," Larry rasps, "we can do with it as we please."

"Really?"

"We work when we want to. Christ, yes." A grin spreads across his broad, tanned face. The other planters grunt to themselves. Larry leans against his shovel looking up at the woodpecker and he talks in a long drawn-out way about the reservations at Longlac and Sioux Lookout, and about fights they've had with the RCMP.

Hate passes around from generation to generation, I must know.

Do the Native officers among the police mean well? "Nothing ever changes," Larry grates.

The crew-bosses are on our backs, they want us to plant trees with no roots sticking out. The woodpecker's rat-tat-tat again. *Vietnam, ah.* My own play-acting with the shovel in my hand— being a vicarious soldier, and I fire!

Larry grins.

The draft-dodgers, Americans—now tree-planters—throw hand-grenades in the air, a whole bundle of trees at a time. One guffaws. Freedom in the Northern Ontario air! Some are, well, seeking nirvana in an ashram not far away. A Mother-Goddess figure with long black hair is their guru, a Kali figure-cum-Durga. My own mother and grandmother back there in the tropics I think about.

Larry watches me scuff the topsoil once more. Real Mother-Earth. Uphill, then downhill over more burnt-out areas we are. Another woodpecker rat-tats away. "We work when we want to, Christ, yes." Larry sniffs the air bracing against a tall birch and he pees. Leaves glisten. The draft-dodgers, calling out that they would rather be in Southeast Asia. *Really?*

"They can be cannon fodder all they want," Larry snorts. "Now it's time to plant the goddam trees!" He points at a bear in the sky, sure. The Crees move in single file. "Shit, do we have to plant these trees?" someone yells.

"The trees must be in the ground," Larry rails. "Yeah, let's get on with it. If we don't plant the trees, who will?" He shrugs, pointing to the other planters imagining being in 'Nam.

"Those bastards," Larry points to the Americans again, "they're hiding the trees." A planter will dig a hole in the ground and bury an entire bundle, then plant a single seedling on top of it, I know.

"What d'you think, eh?" Larry snaps at me.

"Think?".

He tears into the ground, scuffing the earth with his large boots. "Come on, keep planting, it's no time to waste," he bolsters.

Grenades going off. Smoke spirals in air, in all of 'Nam. Whose turn is it now to start another forest-fire? *Christ, no!*

That evening back at camp Larry looks warily at me from across his bunk, and he will once more talk about the reservations. "See, the Third World's here with us," he claims. *Third World?* I tell him of the back-breaking work people do back there—cutting sugar-cane—a far cry from fishing in pristine Canadian rivers as I'd looked at in glossy tourist magazines. And skiers going down BC mountains at breakneck speed, like in my wish-fulfilling moment. British Columbia...New Brunswick, Prince Edward Island, Nova Scotia, Quebec—*here I come!*

Larry goes on about the reservations in Longlac and Sioux Lookout. The Great Spirit hums in my sleep that night. The bear in the sky. *Believe me.*

"Believe you?" Larry snaps.

In the off-season he won't plant trees, but drift off to Toronto, panhandling in the hottest part of summer while living on Yonge Street. And one time when a Swedish chick (he calls her), a blonde—came and she wanted to find out everything there's to know about Native people.

She'd listened to everything he said, like gospel truth.

"Sure, I told her all she wanted to know about natives, dammit. We became a twosome after a while." *In...love!* Larry, you macho-Native shithead! "I told her I wanted to live in Scandinavia. But she said there's no such place." Then, "What about the Vikings I asked her? Heck, she figured I didn't need to know that history."

Larry makes up stuff as he goes along. But my mind flits back to the tropics with a sugar-plantation world in the background. The Hare Krishna types now in Northern Ontario in more time to come.

***

At the makeshift pool-table at camp we keep being who we are, like making up for lost time. And that evening Larry will snore again, maybe because of all the lies he keeps telling me.

But he's the fastest tree-planter around when he gets to it. Heavy boots tramping on the ground in darkness. The next morning's wake-up call from the bull cook once more—yes, Jimmie. We will trudge along in the forest layered with muskeg on swampy ground. I sink knee-deep in muck and grime!

Larry yanks me out. "Come on, there's trees to plant," he yells.

I yell back at him.

He leans against his shovel, the bag slung across his shoulder primed with spruce and pine seedlings. I know he's planning to leave us; and the crew-bosses are anxious about him. He openly mocks their "scientific knowledge" of how long it will take for the trees to grow.

"That's bullshit!" Larry cries.

"What is?"

Guffaws, as the draft-dodgers laugh. *Shangrila...where?*

Larry plants by taking longer steps; and soon after it's no time to take a break, not to light a cigarette—no-one's allowed to smoke in the forest anyway. I try to keep up with him, planting faster. The others do too, Ojibwas...Crees.

Sweat pours down Larry's grizzled face; he wipes it away with his frayed cotton sleeves. No sooner the trees in his bag are gone. The ground throbs as he pounds at it with his hard-boots. Clods of dirt fly in the air; it will take a veritable storm to blow away the trees he's planted—a real northern tornado.

Blackflies by the thousands swirl; the heat becomes intense. "You okay?" he asks me.

He drifts off to plant by himself. Odd, I think I'm at the mercy of bears, moose. Wild horses, also...there are tracks of them.

Where's Larry now...hiding among thorns, rhododendron on this bloodstained ground. A moose's antlers nailed to a great hall somewhere. The hunters from Duluth, Minnesota who'd been here, don't I know?

Drew, a crew-boss, sniffs around, looking for buried trees. He has threatened Larry before, see. He pulls up roots, then a tufted bundle from the ground. He spreads the roots out like a victory trophy and gloats. Ah, Larry had buried an entire bundle.

Is it why he finished planting his trees quickly? I saw Larry plant each tree, I swear. He's our best planter. Tell the crew-boss this.

"The Native bastard, they're all like that. They're the ones setting the fires in the first place so they can get work here each spring and fall," said Drew.

"Not true!"

"I've been looking at him with binoculars."

"No!"

Rat-tat-tat—gunfire—and grenades thrown high in the rancorous air against a russet-hued sky. I'm also taking part in a bear-walk in the clouds. *Larry, you bastard!* "He might be gone now," I say.

"Gone?"

"You were going to fire him anyway."

"No, I was only kidding. The trees have to be planted; we have a quota to fill."

Larry's already in a faraway reservation, like LongLac. The forest's silence grows heavy. Leaves of individual trees rustle; it's another vertiginous moment. *Larry, are you gone?*

***

Back at camp close to Lake Mackenzie, I wonder what's in store for me. "See," Larry said, "you've got to take your chances." Lake water lapping, and bass or pike mirrored, almost like fish spirited out of the sky. My own shaman's sense now.

Larry adds, "The trees, they will rise up from the ground before long, so keep planting. Soon you will be living in a highrise place, don't forget." *Forget?*

"Plant the trees well, mark my words." The Swedish woman's voice… somewhere. Who's racing through the forest, hard-booted and all, as I see trees miraculously coming after me. A bear literally walks across the sky. Before me I only see Larry's footprints.

I will meet him again panhandling on Yonge Street…as time will expand before us. Not in Saskatoon or Winnipeg…or Ottawa. Not in Scandinavia! Sure, I will meet him somewhere in a commonly named Bay Street. *You?*

But he doesn't recognize me.

Somewhere a Swedish woman's voice, yes…who's really writing a book, insisting on all there's to know about Canada's native peoples. She flicks blonde hair from her eyes.

Larry waves to me because of the Great Spirit—as I keep looking back, and indeed it's for me to tell everyone who he really is. Rat-tatting…gunfire. The Great Spirit, see. How much farther north do I go, with voices calling out to me?

Cane-fires burning because of where I've come from, ah. Tourist magazine images appearing and disappearing; and once in a while I will look back at my mother and grandmother, *Shangrila...home!*

MAKING IT

Across a short expanse of brush the partridge hopped, then darted across the moss towards a cluster of spruce and pine here in Quetico Park about fifty miles from Atikokan where we indeed were. With hard boots on I stomped on the soil, then one more tree into the ground I planted. I tugged at it, making sure no roots stuck out. A rhododendron a few feet over I looked at, and I expected to see the partridge scuttle again.

I was also on the lookout for bears, moose. Jim and Steve, the crew-bosses, were behind a clump of bushes...looking, yes, lording it over us. Other planters like Chin, Ossie, and Murph lingered a few yards behind. Who were *stashing* trees? I whipped out another spruce seedling from my bag. And the forest fires... who really set them?

Mickey, a Cree, shrugged; he'd been meditating on the Great Spirit, the bear in the sky, he called it. At the makeshift pool hall at the camp near Lake Mackenzie he would watch me play table tennis, how I banged the ball around, and he laughed.

The day's work was done; and we started trundling home.

"To think we've been here this long," said Chin, an engineering student with short-cropped hair from Djakarta who was planting trees for the first time. Murph, "a Thunder Bay Canadian," growled about not needing the money...three-cents a tree piece work; but he simply wanted to plant trees. I also prided myself planting trees.

Murph sneered. Mickey looked almost savagely at him.

We ploughed through muskeg and slapped at more mosquitoes and blackflies. "Will you come again next season?" asked Murph.

Who...me?

"Maybe," I said.

The cold late September mornings with the planters rising early upon hearing the bull cook's clock-work call followed by bell-ringing; I reminisced about it. Mickey muttered, "No one ever gets used to it."

"Maybe you will," Murph growled,

Mickey's eyes grew incandescent. "Indians are not lazy," he snapped.

Murph whirred, "I didn't say that."

I kept thinking how Steve, the crew boss, earlier that day had come from behind a clump of bushes figuring Mickey was stashing trees—burying a whole bundle at a time with one small tree planted on top; and who would suspect him? Sometimes he threw a bundle up into the overhanging branch of a tall oak, as a foil.

I shook my head.

Mickey said I shouldn't worry about Steve, the Lakehead University fart. He spat on a rotten beech stump. He'd been planting for years, and he was the fastest among us. *But how fast?*

Crew-boss Steve didn't believe him.

Mickey would return to the reservation soon where he drank a lot. Longlac...or Sioux Lookout awaited him with friends, relatives, all who hated the RCMP, calling them "Pigs." Mickey knew every twig, branch, muskeg, in the forest. But he was no trapper, and maybe he'd been a "Native guide" once or twice.

Murph tried keeping up with Mickey, and he breathed in hard.

Chin blithely said, "I'd like to be a trapper someday."

Ossie shrieked, "What for?" Then, "Do they have beavers in Djakarta?" He grinned, adding that he was horny. And was Chin ever horny...back there? *Where?* Chin made a grating noise.

Murph laughed. He often planted close to Mickey, who was irritated by something or the other. Murph kept laughing and walked ahead of us. Chin made a gargoyle's face as he grunted. Murph kept on laughing and crunched down on fallen leaves. He swatted at mosquitoes and loudly swore.

Camp awaited us after the day's work was done. Bites from insects blocked the pores in our skin. I needed a good washing, Murph simply swore, and no one knew what was on his mind.

At camp by Lake Mackenzie, the black water being cold the first time you got in. Fellas lingered on the dock hewn out of birch and pine, glad to be back at the camp. Who would first go in for a swim?

Who...? someone called out. *Who...what?*

Yeah, no matter how tired we were, fellas would just dive in because of the refreshing feel of lake water. Murph laughed. Chin's eyes widened, tropical waters still in his veins. Mickey quickly stripped down to his waist, swarthy-skinned and all; and he was no Metis, we must know.

Murph also stripped down...blond-looking.

The others looked at the lake's water, so inviting.

Ivan, Ossie, and Harold dove in and started swimming, then floated among clusters of vegetation like the tufted water-hyacinths. The tropics again...I reflected.

Standing on the dock, I poured water over my body. Oh, I yelled out that the water was damn cold! A collective squeal, and more splashing noises with the great sky above. Taller spruce, birch, fir, beech...all of Quetico now really with us.

We were here four weeks already, and we boasted about how many trees we'd planted. Sure, who planted the most...not buried the most?

Murph hurled more water, cascading it over his body. He grinned, wide-gummed. Ossie mimicked him. Someone cried out a dare: "Let's swim across the lake!" *Really swim across?* The horizon...a far sky; and after the long day's work was done! I vaguely thought about. Djakarta...Amazon Guyana, the Caribbean. Real voices in my ears.

Murph glanced around, then again looked at me for some special reason. He turned to look at Mickey. "Let's swim across," he challenged us. "We can't, Murph," someone shot back, "not after working all day planting the fucking trees!"

"Why not?" rasped Elmore, a sandyhaired youth from Atikokan who boasted that his family came from Saint John, New Brunswick.

Chin grinned, looking across the lake, the dark blotch of vegetation far ahead in the declining sun; he waved...to no one in particular. "It's more than two hundred yards wide," said Ossie, water cascading over his body as he washed himself.

Others called out an invitation, "Who will really swim across with us?" "Who will?" Murph said and looked at us standing on the dock and feeling tired. *Looking at me?* Mickey was worried.

Elmer reacted, "I will!"

"Who else will?" shrieked another.

Blackflies, mosquitoes, and fish in the lake in dizzying spirals. The water appeared blacker, colder. Shale, rocks, sheer stones. A canoe...someone drifting out. Smithy—an old planter—hailed us; after supper he would take us out to "look around" the edges of the lake. Frogs hiccoughed. Crickets metallically cheeped, mating calls all. Loons cried louder.

Mickey washed away dirt from his ears, and he hissed a command, "Who'll really swim across, eh?"

"Cowards," barked Ossie; and the others smirked.

I thought of supper, spare ribs, potatoes, chocolate-cake dessert; they fed us well. "Come on," yelled Murph, diving in in a long smooth action.

Ah tomorrow, the trees to plant, with each of us being asked to do about fifteen hundred each day. "It's a quota," warned the Camp Superintendent, Mr Blaine...calling us city-slickers.

Ossie, Chin, Brian, Elmer were now ready to start swimming across the lake. A tall spruce wavered ahead, it actually did. A woodpecker rat-tatted louder as other noises commingled.

"Come on," a voice called out to me. Then, "You too, Mickey, Indian as you are!" *Who's a real Indian?* Mickey looked across the lake with the sun in the far horizon, the clouds with vermilion and russet hues. "We can make it," hollered Murph, tongue stretching out.

Someone else laughed, then said, "I'm too goddam tired!"

The woodpecker's assault on birch grew louder. Fish in dizzying spirals, the water everywhere in my line of vision. The urge in me now to simply join the others to really swim across the lake. *A dare, no?*

I was feeling dead-tired.

***

Mickey swam next to me, then slowly moved ahead in his determined crawl. The others, three, four...also moved ahead. The water felt warm in the remnant sun, and I tried to keep up with everyone. I also looked up, then down...below me...my head sometimes bobbing. The land, trees, the wilderness of sky. I threw one arm after another in my special swimming motion. Stygian waters below.

The others left standing on the dock waved, urging us on.

Elmer, he changed his mind...he stood on the dock alone now. A blurred vision. Everyone was now making, well, longer strides, swimming on. I gulped in air and swallowed water.

Mickey almost turned round, but only looked sideways, at me, but he moved ahead. Almost halfway across the lake we seemed to be; and I began to feel a strange headiness.

I threw my arms out harder, and kept kicking out. The trees I'd planted I thought about...as the others moved farther ahead, Mickey more than the others; and maybe everyone figured I was taking my time swimming...as I kept falling behind.

Mickey urged me on, I could tell: "Swim faster!"

Murph moved ahead too, maybe saying, *This isn't as hard as it looks.* Pain in my legs, a calf muscle's twitch and ache; it stiffened.

Suddenly I couldn't swim anymore; as the others kept moving ahead.

Agonizing pain I felt, and with each stroke I made I was starting to cramp up, my leg muscles tightened. *Oh God!*

I started panicking. What was below...how deep the lake?

Mickey, can you see or hear me?

Murph, Ossie, and Chin moving against the sun's vermilion and russet hues, and shades of pink, yellow. A prismatic sheen. Now I was somewhere in the middle of the lake...alone...writhing with pain. I vaguely saw the others on the dock playfully shoving one another into the water, horsing around: Elmer more than the others; he was a bad planter, with his trees' roots sticking out. "Fuck the trees! The fire will burn them anyway," he'd cried.

I tried waving...to him, to say that I was in trouble. *Help, Elmer!*

Elmer, there on the dock, only dove in and out; and how many trees would he plant tomorrow? I really wanted to swim back to the dock...as Chin, Ossie, Murph, Mickey moved ahead towards the opposite bank.

I gulped in water; I must balance my body, and keep floating, even wriggle like a fish...or worm. The pain grew excruciating, I didn't want to die...not drown here in a far northern land in such cold water! God, I would never want to try swimming across the lake again. I would leave the bush camp, leave all of Quetico. The woodpecker's rat-tatting sound in my ears.

I would go back to where I came from...the far tropics. Chin, d'you hear me? Djakarta...how really far away? I again saw the others on the dock, if vaguely, and their applause it sounded like. Was I coming back, and getting closer?

Someone on the dock pointed, and he indeed laughed. *Elmer...you!*

Crew-boss Steve sneered because I was unable to swim across, he was gloating. I pushed on, with the strange power of trees all around. Spruce, pine, birch. Fish, too, an entire school, pushing me, I was making it.

I felt another stab of pain. *Oh God!* One more push...or pull... and the clouds coming down. Sheer forest, insects; and mosquitoes taking out large chunks of flesh from me. Arms flailing, fluttering, then I slapped the water. "Help!" I let out.

I wanted to make it back on my own, a strange pride in me; I'd reach the dock without anyone's help. Mickey, d' you see me now from the other side of the lake? *Murph, d'you, also?*

Someone, on the dock standing ramrod straight began saying: "Look at him, he couldn't do it!" *Yes, me.*

"No...he couldn't!"

I floated along; and it didn't matter where the others were now, if they'd already reached the other side of the lake. *Mickey, are you really there?*

I slowly managed to reach the dock where I'd started from. With pain I spluttered...something, and tried scrambling up. Two or three others came to me, they saw the agonized look on my face.

"You...okay?"

"No, er...yes."

"You sure?"

I nodded.

"But you couldn't swim across, eh?" Laughter, Elmer's.

The others resumed their horsing around, going in and out of the lake. I looked far across; as *they* waved to me. Mickey was smiling. Then they started swimming back...Murph was once more in front.

I lifted my head to get a better view. I heard Murph say...*what*... to me?

"It was easy, see."

Yes.

***

Mickey was alone with me, his face suffused-looking. "I shouldn't have attempted it," he said. *Why not, Mick?* The forest expanding, or converging. "It was difficult, see." *How really difficult?*

I nodded.

Chin, Ossie, Brian congratulated each other; they'd conquered the lake, they said. Murph laughed loudest. Mickey, well, he sensed my anxiety. "No one ever conquers the lake," he said.

Murph also looked at me, as if he knew what I was thinking.

Mickey said, "I shouldn't have tried it," and he stared at Murph.

I felt I was somehow still in the middle of the lake, in one spot. And the next day we'd plant more trees than usual, in rougher terrain. Burnt-out ground with stumps sticking out amidst heavy charcoal everywhere. A muskeg swallowed my boots in!

We scarcely said much to each other. I only concentrated on planting the trees—work that had to be done. I wondered who would *stash* the next bundle...almost before a crew-boss's eyes.

A woodpecker rat-tatted away. Sitting on a log with the others, I listened as Mickey said we needed a break. Another partridge scuttled across the brush. He didn't want to plant anymore, he would stop when he felt like it: his way of saying it wasn't only the white man's way.

He lit a cigarette, though it was forbidden to smoke in the forest. The light illumined Mickey's face. Ah, he knew what I was thinking even as he looked up at the designs in the sky. A hawk or some other bird, somewhere.

Murph said, "Come on, guys, get the hell on with it!"

Speaking to Mickey alone, he was. Then...to me, and my imagining the lake only, and another spare-ribbed supper, the best we would ever eat. Now who would dare to challenge us to swim across the lake again?

Chin laughed. "It's the same in Djakarta, no one wants to plant the goddam trees!"

Mickey kept thinking about the lake. Yes, swimming to the opposite bank, same as Murph. And I was indeed somewhere in the middle with them. Furls of water, and a hazy horizon, tinted-looking, then becoming dark-grey. A far sky, my being in a wilderness, believe me.

FORGOTTEN EXILES

A writer is a world trapped in a person.

—Victor Hugo

I was meeting him again after a twenty-year lapse, and I figured he would be reluctant, too self-conscious to meet me, my father. Time and distance, between us; and maybe it was because of his poverty, his house being a ramshackle place with a nondescript living room, and the doors being boards simply tacked together, the roof being zinc sheets piled one on top of the other. He'd been ailing too, arthritis wracking his bones, the relatives said.

I trudged along a once-familiar winding back road, and my being finally *home*. "I'm here," I called out, like a game I fantasized playing...with him. "Is not you?" came a reply, his familiar voice, a crackle; and he'd been expecting me, as he ambled to the front yard.

His appearance hadn't changed much as he looked out from his gate into a narrow alleyway, in crepuscular light. *Really you?* "You know who it is?" I called out.

"You!" He came closer, almost with a strange doubt.

Mosquitoes buzzed; but he didn't mind the insects, he was inured to them, the way I never was. His familiar hammock on the porch I looked at; and his wife was close by, almost wizened-looking. The few letters between us over the years came back to me: one, in particular, with a photograph he'd sent me, showing real grit on his face. His limbs seemed twisted when they'd once looked strong. His other children came around with their desultory expressions; and my own mother, well, was distant.

I'd been anxious to meet him, my father.

"It'd be quite a meeting," office colleagues had said with drollness.

It wasn't natural for one to be away from his father for so long. It wasn't *Canadian.* My mute response: "I know."

"Know?"

How would I "perform" when I finally met him? Snow coming down; but the tropics being in my mind, like really being in another world...to these Canadian colleagues.

Impulsively I embraced my father, like we were the only father and son in the world now. Mosquitoes buzzed, and I slapped at my elbow. My father's once proud face I looked at closely. His eyelids quivered.

"I missed you, son," he said.

"I missed you too."

His wife appeared in a crevice of light from the porch, shy-looking. I glanced into the living room, as my father beckoned. He owned a TV set—his watching black-and-white shows only, he and his wife viewing American soap operas, but not CNN newscast. And when I'd lived in the village I was fixated on the radio; there was no TV then.

My father knew what was occurring in the "outside world"; goings-on in America, Europe, Russia, Iraq...Afghanistan, all that he saw on the TV screen, and he might have been mesmerized.

And he often wondered how our kind of people came to be here in the Amazon...far from India.

He nodded.

I nodded back. And details of his life: how he lived, and the few heads of cattle he owned. I saw him muttering about how our forebears came from a place called Uttar Pradesh, almost unreal. But, we were here now. His eyes gleamed. And what did he really contemplate as he watched his cows grazing in the sprawling savannah some miles from the village?

He no doubt also wondered how I coped in the "Arctic," meaning Canada, as he wiped perspiration from his brow in the tropical heat. *How did I really?*

His wife, in an angle of light, forced a smile. She was a religious woman: a Muslim, though belief was just that...to assuage or calm the troubled spirit. Calm my father's spirit, too. Now what did he think about in his solitary moments, as he watched the cows graze? And the birds, vultures hovering, forming an arc on the horizon, and thinking about his children, he was. Thinking about *me*, his eldest, living near Lake Superior. He smiled, because of changing circumstances.

His small house was surrounded mainly by mango trees; and his other children lived their meagre lives in fretful ease. Their names, I hardly knew...or, remembered, almost like what my father didn't want me to know.

More relatives drifted in, all come to see me now. A tall youth drifted in closer: a half-brother, with distinct shadows under his eyes. He could have been *me*, in a manner of speaking. Imagine my father being with him in the savannah as he watched the cattle maunder around. The tall youth with a determined face looked at me...longer.

He asked...what? Not about the Arctic...in Canada where I lived?

A new beginning mixed in with an old ending. He milked cows with my father; and his talon-like fingers, his long arms being gangly. He sold the milk to the villagers, house to house; but the villagers lapsed in their payment—my father said—because they were poor. Village-poor!

My father's wife came closer. Did I need to know all that, I who'd been away so long? The tall youth shrugged. The other children also shrugged. The mango trees around rustled their leaves in cow-dung scented air. Insects buzzed. I looked at everyone's faces; and the air grew more humid. The tall youth answered the few questions I asked.

I sustained the image of him alone in the savannah, this son. And he and my father slept under the stars in this place of the Amazon almost marked out, it seemed; yes, he often stood close to my father in a vigil. *What else do I need to know?* Shadows moved under his eyes, the tall youth's. The savannah with strange-looking birds skirting the air. Turkey-vultures hopped on the ground close to the nervous cows…and everything must eventually die.

He talked, in a slow, deliberate manner—my father. The tall youth's mother, Janie, listened intently. Did the youth want to tell me something? *What?* Other relatives drifted in closer. The one youth was now like the only true son…he and my father being there in the savannah, under the stars. *Tell me more.* Now about what kept "worrying" the cows.

The tall youth grimaced. Oh, about a jaguar.

"It's one we wanted to kill," my father said. *A phantom jaguar?*

Eyes looking at me askance. The youth with long nails glanced around uncomfortably. Did my father really, well, *kill* the jaguar?

He'd wrestled the beast to the ground and finally plunged his long-bladed knife into it, if this could be believed. *Aaaaggh!*

How the cows lowed nervously.

And where was I then, but walking through snowdrifts near Lake Superior.

My father's hands tightened round the beast's neck as it scratched and tore into his flesh. Blood poured. More cows bellowed, a sound unlike how it was when my father brought down a calf for branding. The jaguar being literally the Bengal tiger, a *tiga*, which no Indian maharajah or nawab sitting on an elephant's back could have shot with a blunderbuss. Did I come face to face with such a beast in Canada?

Not a cougar?

83

My father's wife's eyes widened.

The savannah bare. A different spirit now, after the tiga had been killed. The tall son looked at the others around us, then turned to me again. They knew something....*What?* That the tiga roamed the South American savannah and was again coming close to the village.

Laughter; oh, the joke was on me!

My father skittered with a laugh of his own. Deliberately...as if this was what he wanted me to know: that the jaguar had come here to the savannah from the deep hinterland forest...because it recognized *him* from way back. *How true?* And he'd made a plan to lure the beast into a large hole, my father did, and the beast would be trapped...for good.

I listened in awe.

But my father's plan didn't work; not for a clever tiga with the smell of India's Ranthambhore forest in its nostrils—a beast with an instinctual sense of where my father and his family actually came from...and now living in the Amazon basin.

I balked.

Others skittered with laughter. But my tall half-brother was silent. My father went on about the tiga, like his way to bring us closer. What else did I want to believe in? I saw the jaguar tearing into more flesh, a prized bull's only. Then one by one the cows disappeared as my father feared would happen. His tall son feared this, too. The youth's mother, Janie, whirred.

Then, "I was the one who actually killed the tiga," the tall youth said.

"You?"

"Young as I am."

The youth's straggly hair spread out on a narrow face, his nose ridged looking. His eyes bore into me. Did he really kill the jaguar?

He described the tiga's coat with its rosettes of yellow, brown and black; and the beast's mouth, with teeth stuck out like short, sharp spears.

The tiga being there in the Arctic with me too at one time. But it couldn't survive the winter cold; it was no cougar on a mountain slope somewhere in Banff, in Alberta. Or a polar bear swimming amongst ice-floes in Nunavut. Could it have been *transformed?*

The youth kept on about how he and the others had tracked the beast into the coastal savannah after it had drifted away from the hinterland forest. *What else?*

Janie, the mother, drew closer. And what did my father not want me to know? About how the cows sniffed, imitating the tiga, then lowed mournfully! All the while the youth in the open savannah was tracking the jaguar, see. My father said he no longer went to the savannah alone because he feared the tiga's spirit.

I grimaced.

"We wanted to tear its spirit out fo' good," said the youth. "Then roast it over a slow fire, to make sure it was dead-dead." Was it revenge on the tiga because it'd killed so many cattle?

My father's cheeks pulsed.

Once more he said he was glad I'd come home. A strange new pulse-beat, also. Now my father's wife Janie wanted to talk about her new faith: she'd become a Pentecostal Christian. Evangelists were everywhere in the district, did I know?

The youth flicked his talon-like nails. The others grinned, seeing how I was taking it all, a real foreigner. *How real?* Janie continued on about her faith.

Instinctively I moved closer to my father on his hammock, as the tall youth turned away.

"You don't believe it, do you?" my father said.

"Believe?"

"About killing the beast."

He showed me his broken teeth, twisting his mouth at an angle. The coastal belt and the savannah now appeared as one: the Amazon converging. The Badlands of Alberta also close. What I dwelled upon while living in Canada, didn't they know? Reindeer and caribou, and ice-fishing in the Arctic as the sea and ocean drifted up near to the prairies.

The other relatives started walking off, for Janie didn't want them around. She wanted me to be alone with my father, to make up for lost time.

I nodded. My father also nodded.

"It's true," he said.

"What's true?"

About the jaguar: as he might have imagined, if only fanci-fully...as legendary Sivaji of Indian lore. And it was also about the Bengal tiger-spirit!

My father heaved in. His tall son also heaved in.

A prism of light, a slow fire burning. The jaguar's coat flick-ered with rosettes of yellow and black. And the savannah drifted away, like echoes of another place far away, as the cows lowed. The tall youth gestured. My father again nodded.

More images came back, including what the office colleagues in Canada had said to me and laughed, when I didn't expect them to...as I would tell them about the tiga-spirit and India's Bengal tiger being one and the same. *Not in the Sundarbans!*

The one youth looked at me, then again turned to my father.

More shadowy light with the others moving around quietly. Surreally. Janie too moved around; as the cows lowed, being everywhere all at once. Tremor in my veins. Voices, you see, in the cold and ice I also summoned up. *Where was I?*

I closed my eyes, but quickly opened them again. Same as my father did. When he laughed next, I also laughed. And the tall youth started walking away; he had the jaguar spirit in him, you see.

More images... as we kept being apart, but close up. And my mother far-gone, as the sea and ocean moved closer, and the for-est quietly disappearing.

Janie stood agape.

My father turned back to his ramshackle door, as if I hadn't come to see him at all. The horizon bending, north and south, and I kept walking in ice-floes, only close-up, remembering.

THE WELL

P arched his lips were as my father leant forward, bending his head to drink from the artesian well where the ground sloped and almost canted under his feet. He would drink now, for he'd been on the winding road for hours bringing his cattle home. Dark and musky it was, and the animals lowed, straggling along, pulling one way, then another, and maybe they sensed something in the darkness.

A swathe of light filtered in from somewhere. His eyes were playing tricks on him, my father said. Then deliberately he turned on the tap. But *someone* was already there...*drinking*. The hunched form, shoulders stooped; and my father must wait his turn to drink, see.

We waited to hear more...what else he would say.

The one already at the well was taking an unusually long time drinking. And the cattle grew skittish, more than usual. A dog barked, ululation somewhere. An ass's distant, but loud bray. The cows grew more restive. My father muttered to himself. A veil of mist descending.

He rubbed his eyes, he had to drink. *Tell me more, Father.*

Lightly he tapped the one before him at the well who was drinking for so long. A bull pranced impatiently. A tremor in my father, he couldn't fool me, and he wasn't thirsty anymore. The one before him, his shoulders stooped: *Who was he?* My own throat felt dry, like I was the one who was at the well trying my father's patience.

"You taking too long," my father rasped.

To...me!

The bent figure turned slowly. "The face smiled at me," my father said, and he swore, "Manu... no other!"

Really Manu?

"The same I used to know so well," my father said with a strange grin. But Manu had died six months ago, and almost the entire village had attended the funeral, my father being one of the pall-bearers.

How the women wailed, Manu's wife Susheila, especially. Manu had been popular in the village, as everyone knew him. Clods of earth thrown onto the coffin I replayed in my mind. *Thud-thud.* My father's own handful, he really grieved Manu's passing. "You sure it was him?" I asked.

None of us believed him, my father. The twitch of his mouth, his forehead wrinkled, as he looked hard at me.

"But you been thirsty an' tired?" someone else said.

"Something must've been the matter wid you, eh?" another tried.

Then, "How can Manu be drinkin' at the well if he was... *dead*?"

My father shrugged, he couldn't make believers of us.

"Is not true," chimed in another.

"Wha' happened next?" I forced the words out, then laughed.

The others also laughed, like mimicry. "What did you do, Gabe?"

They called him that, my father.

"Were you still thirsty?" came a soft shriek.

My father looked at me as he never did before, then turned and looked at the others, one by one...deliberately.

88

For days after I would see him looking glum, and maybe the cattle were getting to him, becoming so skittish; and this work of bringing them home later in the day on the long, winding road—it really tired him. But something else was on his mind; on all our minds.

The sun's heat beating down, and indeed it was the hottest time of the year. But Manu, I kept thinking about, how well my father knew him. Did Manu really kill himself as had been said? And Susheila had bawled out, I still kept hearing her.

My father walked round the house, looking forlorn in a way I hadn't seen before. Now I wanted to know everything that happened at the well; the water still running, as I shook my head, listening.

My father kept up his silence; he smiled by himself only. I looked away. Odd, I began to harbour a strange fear of him, my father. He sat down with me, us, and muttered something, now to allay my fear.

But something else was really on his mind. Before I knew it, he was gone again, and he seemed not like my father anymore. So strange, whirring in me: this thought.

***

The others kept whispering Manu's name, like a game they were playing...hush-hush. And some told their own stories about the dead, aligned to folklore. Yes, about a man on a white horse riding through the village and dragging a chain behind him...so eerie it sounded.

We grew more afraid each passing day as stories kept coming to us. At night we peeped through jalousies and windows to catch a glimpse of the dreaded spirit. *What spirit?* Sugar-plantation time, ah: alive with the past of slavery, and white planters chasing after runaway slaves on their horses at night. Chains rattled louder.

When the runaway slaves couldn't stand it any longer they gave themselves up because they were so afraid. Heads lowered, sunken, as they returned to do their masters' bidding.

Another tale about an old woman changing her skin, the *ole higue* in our village, indeed the dreaded vampire!

When my father came home late that afternoon, I watched him closely as he mumbled to himself. He sharpened his long-bladed knife, and his lips pulsed; the same knife he carried with him to the backland to cut the thick head-rope he used to lead the cattle home.

He rubbed a calloused finger against the knife's edge to test its sharpness, then he sliced through strands of rope. I watched him intently. And the image of the one at the well returned. *Manu...truly*?

My father was ready to lead the cattle home once more, I replayed in my mind. And one anxious bull jerked left, then right. "Ho boy, ho," my farther called out. "Ho...there!" Did he know something would happen, what no one else did?

Another lore came back: the *moongazer,* a really tall man who only looked up at the moon in his steadfast gaze, and his legs were spread out straddling the street, and whoever passed under him came to his immediate end. *Really*?

My father looked at me, thinking about Manu—he couldn't fool me. He actually saw Manu at the well with shoulders stooped.

"Did you really?"

He didn't answer.

Then, "Did I wha'?"

"See... *him*?"

Manu shouldn't have died the way he did: how he committed suicide; my father moved his lips strangely. See, Manu had really quarrelled with his wife Susheila, as was rumoured. Sometimes he was dressed to kill wearing neatly pressed sharkskin trousers, and he combed his hair straight back with the aid of a thick Brylcreem, Manu did. A Bollywood movie-star he figured he was; but movies weren't made in our village, only in India...far away.

Was Manu disappointed he wasn't living in a place like Mumbai?

Susheila quarrelled with him even more, telling him he was no movie-star! She harangued him about going to work in the canefields. And overnight Manu became gaunt. But some said he'd become plagued by the *ole higue,* the vampire coming to suck blood outa him. Not outa Susheila wth her good looks an' all...as the ole higue was famous for doing to young Indian women?

African belief and lore with us, also, since the time of slavery. *Who really believed anyway?*

How we laughed. I laughed loudest. It was how Indians and Africans lived together, and perhaps we were no longer afraid of the ole higue. *But we were!*

My father hummed, "It was dark, you see." I looked at him intensely. "It wasn't jus' my imagination," he added.

I blurted out, "No, father."

Right then I thought of my mother who'd gone away. And the knife in my father's hand...and the cattle lowing mournfully. The ole higue, where was it now?

My father shook his head. "I know what you thinkin', Son."

His affection was like never before, I wondered; and he would tell me about his own youth and how he'd always tended the cattle and kept going to the backlands before daybreak. He had no choice because it was how our family lived, following a tradition.

***

Once more my father would go to look after the cattle, like my own obsession...and bringing the cows home on a long winding trail. Yes, I was with him, though my father wanted me to stay behind. He didn't want me to become a *cow-man* like him, he said.

My mother said the same; and was it why she'd left?

My father tapped his calloused finger against the blade of his knife; it appeared shiny, lethal. I quickly rubbed my eyes.

"You see," he said, "that well...I passed by it again today, it had no one near it."

"Oh?"

"No one drinks from it anymore, hot as it is."

"Why not?"

He frowned. "Everyone...so afraid now."

"Who...wha' for?"

"That Manu, maybe he's still alive..."

"He cyaan be!"

A dull sound escaped my father's lips, "I was there, see, it was really dark. Just light from de moon...shining a little." He blinked, and crinkled his eyes. He continued, "But I was very thirsty, I had to drink." He stopped, he couldn't go on.

"Go on," I urged.

Long minutes dragged by.

He reminisced: "I was really there when Manu died; I mean, I looked at him...hanging there, looking as if he wasn't really dead." *Go on!* "He didn't want to die. But Susheila, maybe she wanted it to happen."

Wanted...what to happen?

"I saw Manu hanging there, yes, I watched him." He looked unnatural now, my father. Outside in the backyard the cattle lowed mournfully; and something they sensed with their instinct, those animals. Another long night with rain threatening; and stranger it was becoming everywhere.

Heavy drops falling on the zinc-topped houses, and lightning flashed...the equator coming closer. I kept looking out from the window. My father stood next to me, I felt his breath. The animals were really fidgety. The flamboyante and cochineal trees swayed their branches. The knife in my father's hand flickered, the blade luminous in another flash of lightning. Electricity flitted through the windows of our house, believe me.

The knife tearing away flecks of flesh, a young bull's. My father gripped the carcass firmly, then dressed it to perfection. A feast it'd be, a celebration. *A wedding?* Somewhere, my mother's eyes brightened. More I would imagine.

I was the one holding the knife and moving it expertly, tearing away flecks of flesh. Lightning kept flashing. *I saw a face at the window.* Quickly I rubbed my eyes. How the knife-blade glinted in the luminous dark. Then the face disappeared. *Whose was it?*

My father whispered ...something. *What?*

I would sleep soundly that night as the rain kept pounding, like it would never stop at all, it would go on forever.

***

The next morning I went outside the house to see my father at work, the early riser that he was. But he wasn't around. The fresh tropical air I breathed in; the windswept grasses looked greener; the jamoon tree's leaves dripping after the rainfall. The roof of the ramshackle barn also dripped, and the ground everywhere was soggy and wet with puddles. I walked along, hopping over ditches.

The sun started coming out, then really shining. My father with his trousers hitched up to his knees waded through mud and water; he kept goading the animals along as they lowed mournfully. "Ho, boy. Ho, girl," he called out. Then, "G'wan!"

His voice an echo really. He cursed and pulled out his knife, the blade glinting. Hotter it was becoming with long days and nights ahead.

So strange, I was going to the well alone, in broad daylight. I was thirsty, I had to drink.

I threw one leg after another, moving along, being almost in a daze...after bringing the cattle home: like what I had to do. And more thirsty I became, my lips really parched.

On the sloping ground before me at the well I leant forward, hunching my shoulders...and I expected to be stopped because a hand would arrest me. Someone telling me I mustn't drink here!

Manu?

Immediately I wanted my father close by, now more than ever. Overhead cirrus clouds formed. I looked sideways, left and right, and I breathed harder. Sounds of beating hooves, cattle in wild commotion. *Oh, Gawd!* The animals grew wilder...because of my being here now. Trees everywhere shook. My father wielding a heavy rope; and that knife again glinting, you see.

My throat felt more parched.

The rope taut in my hand, as my father stood close by.

Crows circled overhead because of the sun's rays. Arabesqued shadows formed, on the wavering ground. "Father," I called out.

But he wasn't there. An ass brayed louder. The villagers' voices, the mourners being in a procession. *Ah, Manu!*

***

93

Now everyone dared me to call out to my father because he'd been the first to see Manu, incredibly so...after he'd hanged himself. Make no mistake about it! How the villagers jeered, their mouths opening and closing, then expanding like rubber.

My father had indeed seen the dead-alive, seen the *jumbie*, in broad daylight. But he wouldn't tell me, he never really did. Immediately I thought of my mother... where was she now?

Father, I called out, just as he seemed ready to attack the form in speckled white before him with his long-bladed knife; yes, lunge into it. *What...form?*

"It's me," I suddenly cried.

Clouds somersaulted. Crows, vultures, in commotion; beaks and claws everywhere. Everyone's laughter grew louder, then a veritable clamour. Blood poured. This final act, my father's. And somewhere was Susheila. *Manu, where...actually?*

My father hummed, "You see, that night, Manu had been expecting someone to come to the well. Maybe his wife Susheila. A tryst between them, see." Manu, movie-star handsome as he was. Susheila believing that he actually came from Bollywood and was here in our village only for a short while.

My father's eyes burned. Was he thinking about my mother now?

He said, "Manu didn't expect me to be at the well, dead as he was. But he knew...as I knew."

Knew what?

My father added, "Then I pulled out the knife just when he turned around, and I was about to lunge it at him...then he saw me!" My father closed his eyes. "It happened so quickly!" He sucked in air. "I really did; but no-one would believe me, eh?"

Blood, like an ongoing sacrifice. His words, monosyllables. His own rage...with the world...here under the equatorial sun— the more I thought about it, about the life we lived, father and son together.

And my mother, looking almost like Susheila, do you know?.

A white horse kept dragging a chain behind it all night long, somewhere; and the ole higue vampire being still at it, going after young women's thighs…with fresh blood in her veins. *Who… really?*

"They must believe he's real," my father said.

Manu, yes.

"I lunged the knife, but only into thin air," he added, my father, then he stopped and looked at me. "You never forget a thing like dat. *Swoosh….*the knife went in." He gripped me by the shoulder, and it hurt. He would now tell what I really wanted to know. About my mother, gone to a far place…like to India.

"Father?" I rasped.

I was dreadfully alone…at the well, in darkness. Silence only.

Slowly I turned, my hunched form at the well—looking back, expecting to see who…*MANU!*

A FATHER'S SON

L arge, really big his eyes were, Opie's; and they indeed called him that, short for "Opium"—though drug-taking was almost unheard of where we lived, in our district. Opie rubbed his eyes, then looked at you hard, and immediately you wanted to move away from him. But the others around snickered, or simply laughed. More news kept coming to me in Canada—the letters telling me how the family was really doing.

Opie wiping his eyes with frayed shirtsleeves, lips set tight, I thought about; and he may have been born with that name, *Opie*, incredible as it sounded. And Grandma would call out to him from the balcony of the old house built on stilts, *"Come here!"* Then, *"Go there!"* Opie with hair swept back from his face, shirt-tails hanging out, ran to do her bidding; but then he would open his eyes and rub them against his sleeves. Grandma, now an invalid, would shout from the window: "Boy, go an' get de eggs!"

She never called him Opie; and she figured the relatives—an aunt, uncle, and the wayward children around—would steal the precious hens' eggs. Squabbling was common in the household, with Grandma and Opie on one side, and everyone else on the other.

The next letter in my hand I slowly read, and again I heard Grandma bawling: "Boy, hurry up, get de eggs!"

Opie deliberately threw one leg after the other stepping across the yard, loping over tall grass to the chicken-coop as he sidestepped loose boards jutting out at the front and sides. Grandma watched him; and he was the only one who could "cope" with her, it was said, more irascible as she was becoming each day.

Dee—my mother—wrote about Opie's patience with Grandma, and he was put "in charge" of her, for he'd developed a knack for *tolerating* her. But Auntie—Opie's mother—grew increasingly impatient and crochety, especially after her husband had taken off: he sometimes left for days, so unpredictable he was. *More I imagined, see.*

Opie deliberately put a hand under the laying hen, careful to avoid the aggressive beak. It was like I was back "home" watching his every move. Five minutes later with a smile on his face he walked up to Grandma sitting on the porch at the top of the outside stairs. "Where's de egg?" she called out.

"Eh?" he pretended not to hear her, hands kept behind his back; then with glee he walked up the stairs and grinned. "Where's de egg, boy?" Slowly Opie stretched out his hand and put the prized egg before her.

Grandma smiled; and this way they humoured each other.

She said wistfully, "See, your father never takes care o' you the way I do." Opie simply looked at her, thinking...*what?* Then a smile crept across his face. A few seconds later, his eyes widened, in his uncanny way, I figured. Grandma's diabetes was taking its toll. By humouring her, Opie helped her ease her pain, ah.

Grandma rasped, "I'm an invalid now, but it wasn't always so."

Her self-pitying tone, yes. She dropped a tear, being lachrymose. Opie looked down...with his looking-down eyes. Maybe then he thought about his father, an alcoholic and now the butt

97

of everyone's jokes. His father would come back home emaciated-looking. But he was off again in another drunken spell. Opie's mother fretted even more; and Opie would keep away from him. His father would say, haltingly, he only came back home to see him—his son Opie.

Auntie—Opie's mother—simply grew more irritated; and she didn't care much for Opie either. I read the next letter telling me that Opie had "ambition," and he wanted to go some place far…even come to Canada.

Did he really?

Dee, my mother–living in the town–encouraged him, it seemed.

But Opie coming to be with me in Canada was just wishful thinking. Canada with ice and snow was beyond him, I knew.

Grandma again called out: "Opie, where are you? Come here quick, boy!" Immediately he ran up to her…as tears rolled down her cheeks.

Opie patted her hand and said a few "nice" words to her.

Grandma and Opie grew closer—which no-one seemed to understand about the special spirit that grew between them. Ah, everyone thought too about me living in Canada, and about my special fondness for Opie.

Opie was slowly replacing me in Grandma's affections. The next letter fluttered in my hand. More letters came about the other relatives', some being layabouts, who watched Opie and Grandma becoming quite a twosome, they said.

Opie confronted them, protecting Grandma from their jibes, their taunts. Another season of snow—and my indeed being far-away, yet close.

***

Grandma died not long after; and talk began going around about how Opie would have to leave the home due to the wrangling among the relatives—each now laying a claim to Grandma's house.

Auntie grew more estranged from her husband… and from Opie as well. I read the last letter from Dee, about how Opie's father had gone away for good. And the more fair-minded relatives began saying that the house really belonged to Opie!

"He took care of de old lady to the end," grated one. Grandma's last words before she died was her calling out Opie's name.

And did he really want to be with me in Canada? Opie—becoming a grown-up now—wanted to live by himself: to be far from everyone and silently mourn Grandma's passing.

Opie should go and live with my mother, Dee, in the town—not live with his own mother, Auntie. Auntie would yell at Opie, "Go an' find your fader; he shouldn't come back here to live wid me!"

"Eh?" Opie opened his eyes widely.

"Go an' live wid Dee then. She's been the ole lady's special one." Dee was often the butt of Auntie's sarcasm. "Dee has a bakershop in the town—go an' live with her!"

Opie scratched his head, thinking.

"Go... go!" hurled Auntie.

Opie thought of Grandma and the hens clucking.

He really did.

***

My mother had a genuine soft spot for Opie, I sometimes obsessively kept thinking about in Canada. Not long after Opie actually moved from the village to the town to live with Dee. I read Dee's last letter with some anxiety; I waited for another to come.

Sixteen going on to seventeen Opie was. Dee's letter in my hand fluttered. Her reminiscing about Grandma's "good old days," and Opie collecting the eggs for her like a prized specimen. Indeed Grandma had called out Opie's name in her dying moments, Dee wrote.

Opie might have a future working in the family bakershop in the town, Dee concluded. A new life now for Opie I contemplated.

But his quiet manner was baffling, especially to the other workers in the bakershop, other youths...about his age.

"Why he never talk much?" they asked Dee.

Dee wanted me to know all the details. I replied saying I should come home for a visit; to see Opie and figure out how things were shaping up in the family. My reply letter being passed around from hand to hand…about the "Canadian" returning home; and would I tell them about the charmed life I was living in Canada?

Everyone looked at snapshots of me standing close to Lake Superior and swimming amidst ice-floes!

Images circled around; ah, Canada wasn't unbearably hot and humid like the tropics. Laughter as everyone looked at me bundled up in a parka and looking "like an Eskimo," they said. Another photograph showed me riding a skidoo and being snow-covered. How they laughed at this picture.

Opie laughed, too.

I lamented the fact that Grandma wouldn't be around when I returned home. "The Canadian will be really surprised to see Opie now," taunted Dee. "See, he was always keen on teaching Opie how to read well," heckled another.

With Dee's last letter in my hand, I started feeling anxious about coming home. And Opie's father – the drunk – was never heard from again. *Where was he?*

***

When I arrived home I couldn't believe my eyes: Opie appeared to have sprouted overnight, like a tree. Dee hinted that he'd been courting as well, though I would still see him in his shirt-tails. "Opie, my God – how you've grown!" I cried, looking him up and down.

A dim smile creased his mouth. Then it was his looking-down eyes, just as I expected.

One of the town boys near me smirked, "He's now married!"

"Eh?" I couldn't believe my ears. "Really married?"

Opie looked up at me, and nodded.

I met his wife soon after: a wisp of a girl, with a baby in her arms. "Opie—your child?" I cried.

"Yes," came the reply from an onlooker, happy at my continuing amazement—"the Canadian," waiting to be further surprised. Opie's wife had looking-down eyes, also.

I studied them both. "Opie, I can't believe this," I said, and took the child in my arms.

The child giggled.

Opie smiled, the first time I saw him smile like that. His wife smiled, too. "He behaves well," Opie said, referring to the baby.

"How old is he?"

"Four months," said the wife.

Opie must have been very anxious about me seeing him with a wife and child. Now that we'd gotten over that, he would tell me everything that happened while I was away, especially details about Grandma's final days.

Privately I wanted to ask him why he'd gotten married…he, so young; I was the "Canadian," see.

We would watch Opie in the bakershop working with the others, "the town boys" as they were called. Everyone sweltered in the heat coming from the large indoor oven, and the humidity grew tenfold. I was staying with Dee and observing Opie close-up. And what about Grandma's old house in the village?

No one said much about it.

Dee patted Opie on the shoulder, tall and stringy as he now appeared. His wife reached just above his waist, yes. "Why he don't say much I don't know," Dee muttered about Opie's usual silence.

"He's always been like that," I replied nostalgically.

She nodded. "You t'ink is because of Ma?" She meant the old woman (Grandma). "She's had such an influence on him, you know."

I looked at Dee, thinking hard. "I wrote to you about it," she said. "Before she died, she kept bawling out for him."

I nodded.

"The nurses wanted to know who he was. Opie's name being the last on her lips – her last word." Dee wiped away tears, sentimental as she too was.

***

After about one week of my stay, Opie's father appeared from out of the blue almost…to see me, the "Canadian". Really emaciated he looked. He was also aggressive, the result of his alcoholic state no doubt. The workers at the bakershop laughed in their usual manner—they were used to Opie's father's strange behaviour.

Dee simply said he came now to "face me".

I braced myself for what was to come. Then deliberately Opie came out of the bakershop; he looked at his father with his silent looking-down eyes—commanding him to go away.

The next day everyone gossiped about how Opie had "power" to drive away his father. They tittered. But others commiserated, some with mock sympathy. One called out, "Opie, he's still your father, you know. Don't be ashamed of him!"

Opie busied himself putting dough into the oven, perspiring as he worked. His back bare, skin darker; he ignored everyone's taunts.

"You t'ink your father will come again?" another chaffed.

Opie knew his father had come wanting to see *me*. But he was determined to keep his father away from the *Canadian*, no doubt. A mature Opie wanted me to see only the good side of the family.

Dee nodded, and smiled.

***

Opie's father showed up again, as was to be expected. Now he was well-dressed, clean-shaven, a surprise to everyone. A dozen lobsters knotted, strung together, were in his hands. "For you," he said to Opie, handing over the lobsters with his long, thin arms.

"Give them to Dee," Opie replied curtly; and some of the lobsters were meant for me to enjoy, no doubt.

Dee grinned. "I'll make lobster soup. Come an' have some for supper; it will fatten you up," she said, humouring Opie's father. My Canadian presence was having an effect on her, on the entire family.

Opie's father's appearance, I focussed upon. Dee smiled again.

Hari—or *Hairy*, as some called him—grinned uncomfortably. Opie kept up his looking-down eyes only.

Hari rubbed the back of his neck, becoming fidgety. I knew he wanted money to buy Demerara rum…and to him the Canadian was filthy rich. He wouldn't dare ask Opie for money, but with me he had a chance.

"It's lot o' work catching those crabs," he said coyly. "I was up early goin' by the seaside." Again he rubbed his neck, sheer nervous reaction. "I'm thirsty… all that work," he moaned.

I handed Hari all the loose change I had. He grinned, and hurried off.

That evening at supper we tasted the lobsters, which Dee specially cooked by boiling them slowly in coconut milk. I licked my lips, I hadn't tasted such fare in a long time. My thoughts were far removed from Lake Superior and swimming amongst ice-floes.

Dee muttered, "He will never come, it's a good thing," referring to Opie's father. Then she rebuked: "You should never've given him money to buy *poison*." She referred to rum as *poison*.

I continued enjoying the lobsters.

Opie was now ready to go home to his wife and child. He came to say goodbye to me. He looked greasy; but his eyes were alert. "He na come here yet?" he asked Dee about his father.

"It's late," Dee said, handing Opie a few lobsters for him to take home to his wife. "He will come later," Opie said, like a warning—and looked at me. He climbed onto his bicycle and pedalled off, the lobsters banging against the handlebar. He looked back at me, and waved.

"That Opie," said Dee, "how he's grown. But the boys in the bakershop wonder why he never says much. Ma would've been proud of him though." She meant Grandma.

An hour later Opie's father showed up, hands thrust out in the air; he appeared inebriated. "Where's my son?" he demanded to know. "Gone," said Dee, resentment welling up in her.

"He waitin' to see if I come here drunk, I know it! That Opie –it's how he thinks!" He looked menacing.

"He's really gone," I said.

"You lie!" he snapped.

Dee was flustered, though I wanted her to remain calm—the *Canadian* way.

"I mus' have some supper," Hari said and advanced towards Dee.

Dee lashed out: "Opie has taken your share. Go after him, not come at us!"

Hari growled, "I brought lots o' lobsters. Opie can go an' catch his own, the sea's full o' them!" His eyes wavered, and he came closer; he kept shaking.

A small crowd gathered – neighbours, passersby – watching Opie's father's antics and ready to laugh openly. Others wanted a scene to occur so as to tease Opie about it the next morning...and to tease me, also.

"Get out of here!" cried Dee.

Hari stood his ground, hands akimbo. "I mus' see my son first; I want to tell him what's on my mind!"

"What's on your mind?" Dee advanced towards him.

Everyone laughed, seeing amusement in Dee's threatening action. She hissed back, to me, "He's always been like dat – a mad man!"

I felt a strange pity for Opie's father; and maybe for Opie, too. Then sadness, the frustration building up—what I wasn't ever exposed to in Canada. The onlookers laughed, some applauding.

I really wanted Dee not to react to the crowd's playful taunts; but she cried out, "He mad, really mad – all these years he's been like that," as if to say I shouldn't have gone to Canada and left her alone to deal with the family's problems.

The next morning Opie heard about his father's behaviour. "Opie, those lobsters, they were crawling inside him everywhere," one youth taunted. "They jumpin' in an' out of his eyes all the time," laughed another.

Opie's concentrated on his work of baking bread shoving the large cast-iron tray with dough deep into the wide oven. Heat swirled around him. "Is that why your mother lef' he for another man, Opie?" another jeered. Opie seethed.

I moved close to him; I watched him put the white dough shaped like eggs into the oven, so busy he was. "Hey, take it easy, Opie," mocked another. Then, "He's your father, don't be ashamed of he!"

"I'm not ashamed!" Opie snapped back, and he perspired even more.

The others snickered louder.

Dee said to me, "That Opie, I wonder what he thinks about". I shrugged. "He's like that all the time. One day he will do something," she said ominously. *Something?*

An older worker said: "He can really bake though, for a village boy." "But his father," chided another, "he don't like to see Opie doing that."

I reflected on Grandma again, what she'd once told me—kept urging me, "Son, try and make him learn, or else he'll have no future."

I'd tried tutoring Opie, but he wore my patience.

"That Opie," said Dee, "he can bake better than all these town rascals. They only listen to reggae an' thinkin' they're Rastaman now."

Opie wiped his forehead, and smiled. He knew I was watching him, in a manner of speaking.

***

My three-week stay was coming to an end; it was time to return to Canada. Opie and his wife came to see me off—for the "last time," as they referred to it. Canada was a far place away, and I was going back there.

Opie wore a neatly pressed flower-patterned shirt, which he was careful not to get creased; he kept an eye on the cuffs. "I'm glad I've seen your son," I said to him. His wife smiled.

"When you coming back?" Opie asked, doubtful.

"I don't know. Another three years, maybe."

Opie forced a smile. His wife also smiled. "He will be grown then. When you come back he'll not recognise you," she said, referring to her infant. Opie had his looking-down eyes, ah.

Right then Opie's father appeared, as if he hadn't recovered from his last bout of drunkenness. "Ha-ha," he revved up, "my son will still be here when you return, still in the bakershop working like a *slave*."

"Slave?" Dee snapped. Then, "Leave him alone!" By "him" she meant me, of course. "He doesn't want to hear your mad talk, you are drunk!" She was becoming more flustered. Opie's father sometimes had this effect on her.

Hari snickered. "You go see, that Opie," he pointed. "Thinks he's a grown man; he should be living with me instead of dat old woman. She's dead now. Everyone will soon be dead!"

"Get out!" snapped Dee.

"You... too... dead!" He pointed a bony finger.

Opie's child began crying, suddenly bawling out. Some of the youths around grimaced because of the ugly scene developing.

"You mustn't come here again," cried Dee, advancing towards the bony finger. Like a medieval play being acted out it was, with Opie's father in the role of the grim reaper.

Opie's father stood his ground against Dee. I shuddered. Just when the situation seemed to get out of hand, Opie slowly came out of the bakershop, his eyes having a strange leaden power in them.

Opie's father stood still. The infant stopped crying. All waited to hear what Opie would say in the silence that followed. His father's bony finger lowered, the drama's anti-climax. Everything began to seem, well, "normal" again.

Dee breathed a sigh of relief. Looking at Opie, then at his father retreating, I also breathed a sigh of relief. I was now ready to leave for Canada to be near Lake Superior amidst ice-floes. I'd be gone for another four or five years, but my thoughts would be on Opie all the while with Grandma and hearing her call out *Go on, get the eggs, boy!*

Opie looked at me, and maybe he genuinely wanted to be with me in Canada to swim amongst ice-floes. And another letter in my hand...as I would also see Opie's father somewhere far... smiling to himself. *When will you come home again?*

LEOVSKI'S BLUES

*L*eovski Donov my brother called himself, and he was really pleased as he drew a picture of himself being Lenin with chin and goatee jutting out reflecting the revolutionary's iron will. Next he started writing poems: none of your bourgeois preoccupation with self-reflection, or about a pastoral nature which our local poets were good at. Leovski's poems were about struggle and exploitation, what the workers wanted to hear—poems he read out loudly to himself and recorded. He also wrote essays extolling progressive forces, you see. When Cuba's revolutionary *Granma* came, the weighty newspaper the postman brought to our home, his eyes lit up; the postman would cast a glance back at him, suspiciously.

Genuine Russian Leovski wanted to be; and he hoped his essays about Marxism and Third World socialism would be read by all, especially if he published them in American magazines like *The Village Voice* and *Harper's*.

I began to become worried about him, my brother. Other people were also going through "transformation," those who

107

changed their names by adopting authentic African ones as the back-to-Africa movement grew. Marcus Garveyism spread everywhere. For my brother, though, being a Russian was all despite our Indian tradition. I simply humoured Leovski, and smiled.

He didn't.

My mother grew worried, sensing what was going through his mind. When I saw Leovski leading a long line of "peasants and workers," each waving a placard, I became more concerned. I tried talking Leovski out of his revolutionary zeal. By now the name *Leovski Donov* was being bandied about…not without some awe.

He also inspired jest: the word *Leovski* written down as graffiti on street-side culverts and cowpens. But it was my brother's popularity, if mixed with ridicule, I figured.

A couple more marches on the main road and our entire family became worried. My mother, unlettered as she was, asked me where he got the name *Leovski Donov* from.

I chuckled.

My youngest brother Dev called out playfully, "*Le-ov-ski,*" like a song. Others picked up the refrain. But Leovski held his chin straight, real Lenin-like. We must get rid of poverty once and for all, he declaimed, then harangued everyone about the difference between idealism and materialism. He struck an intellectual pose; he played a tape-recorder "practising" his speeches that he would soon deliver to his "comrades".

"D'you really mean that, Leovski?" I asked sceptically.

"Exploitation must soon end!"

"What exploitation?"

He shrugged, and became disgusted with me.

By now a few "progressive" youngsters in the district were being sent abroad by the Party; and when they returned they peppered their conversation with words like "dialectical materialism" and "scientific socialism"—which would end Third World exploitation once and for all.

Leovski going abroad too, I imagined, and when he returned he'd never be the same again. In Moscow I saw him calling everyone *tovarish* (comrade)—as he urged real social change. Russian hardliners listened to him with curiosity. Sure, they agreed with Comrade Leovski Donov. Communist International was on the right track, my brother being in the "vanguard."

Leovski showed the Russians his essays – articles all written long hand. And with verve he talked about workers everywhere being exploited—like they were an abstract breed—not locals who sometimes guffawed at the slightest joke and were bawdy, or sometimes roguish.

His audience listened to him; and they repeated the name *Leovksi Donov*, even as they focussed on his Hindu features. My brother went on to expound on the differences between pragmatism, idealism, and materialism—nothing rhetorically nuanced about him. He was in the vanguard, see.

My mother moaned once more.

Leovski insisted that I must also call him "comrade"; and he quoted Marx, emphasizing that Marxism-Leninism wasn't a dogma, but "a guide to action".

"Are you sure about that, Comrade Leovski?" I tried mocking him.

He scoffed.

"We're not in Russia, you know."

"We could be," he shot back.

I forced a smile.

"Progressive forces will survive. We must have international solidarity," he went on.

My mother became troubled. Now I had to steer my brother back on the right path, if only for our mother's sake. Before I knew it she too began calling him "comrade" then by his made-up Russian name— not his real Hindu one, *Doodnauth*.

"Leovski," I growled, observing how his eyes twinkled.

Yes, he gloated; he was triumphant.

I was flabbergasted.

***

I started making plans to come to Canada, to attend university. Leovski said that Canadian education was bourgeois: it didn't prepare one to bring about world revolution and end poverty. I knew he'd say that because of his political zeal.

He sneered at me. But he was my brother, and I was glad he had ambition. Leovski turned away from me, now to talk to the sugar-cane workers who came to consult him about something or the other, maybe to plan another protest march. And everyone wanted to develop new "strategy and tactics" to confront the capitalists.

I watched Leovski become more animated, even comical when he waved his arms about and swung them like windmills. I recalled when we were children and visited relatives on the Corentyne Coast close to the Atlantic how everyone doted on us, and on my brother especially because of his wavy hair and hand-some looks.

He might become a movie-star one day, Bollywood being on everyone's mind. Didn't they think he would become a revolutionary?

I remembered when we were coming home from the Corentyne travelling along a winding road in a bus oddly named *Duke of Kent* (another was called *Lord Mountbatten*) and the bus horn blew loudly, my brother trembled, the seven-year-old that he was; and the live chickens the relatives had given us were ready to fly out from our hands! The bus's passengers looked at us worryingly, as pandemonium grew.

I would remind Leovski about this incident. "Those chick-ens," I prompted. But he was only ready to give another speech to the workers and peasants. He shook his fist and quoted facts and figures to his audience; where he got his statistical information from I didn't know. He often made notes, the statistics he copied down, which he then read into a tape-recorder.

The postman came again and handed him another parcel from Havana. *Granma:* more propaganda material, though Leovski never called it that.

"You better be careful," I said to him, knowing the govern-ment didn't take kindly to dissidents.

He simply called me the "Canadian"—because I was thinking of going abroad. Odd, I began to admire how he spoke and gesticulated before an imaginary audience. A nephew or niece would sit with me—whom I nudged at to listen carefully to Leovski about forming a "dictatorship of the proletariat". The workers and peasants applauded.

I raised a hand at the back of the peasants' group meeting to challenge Leovski about one point or other; but he again dismissed me— the "Canadian". Right then the image of my brother as a child came back: he in the bus and trying to hold down the chicken for dear life's sake…as *Duke of Kent* thundered down the Corentyne roadway.

And would the chicken escape from his hands and fly from seat to seat with everyone trying to grab it? "We'll soon be home," I tried soothing him. "Hold the hen down firmly."

"It go bite me!" he cried.

"No!"

He clamped the chicken between his legs, and maybe his activism began at that moment.

I wanted to tell his audience of workers and peasants about this incident, and hear them laugh. Leovski glared at me. One worker gave me a nudge – wanting me to listen carefully to Leovski's revolutionary talk. After everyone congratulated him, pumping his hand as if it'd never stop.

Again I imagined Leovski meeting one Communist leader after another in Moscow; then it'd be Fidel Castro in Havana. Comrade Fidel with cigar sticking out of his bushy beard also pumped his hand, calling him *companero* (something like that). Castro also whispered the name of Che Guevera…as if Che and my brother were on equal terms.

"The Third World must never succumb to American imperialism," Castro said, and my brother nodded approval.

"We mustn't allow ourselves to become like Grenada and Panama," Castro continued, brandishing his hands.

Leovski grinned.

I too grinned, "Canadian" as I was.

***

"Leovski Donov," I whispered the name to myself in our kitchen, reminiscing. My mother heard me, and frowned. Din-

111

ner-time, and my brother joined us in our small house, hungry as he was after the energy he expended making speech after speech. But he looked at the pot of simple food, well, disdainfully.

"You must eat, Leovski?" my mother urged.

"Hurry up then," he commanded as she dished out the rice— he wanted a special helping—with an assortment of curried vegetables and dhal.

"When's your next meeting, Leovski?" I teased.

He didn't answer.

"When are you meeting the workers?"

"Soon," he bolstered; but he also looked away...because something else was on his mind. He looked sternly at me, as if ready to quote more statistics. But stuffing his mouth full of rice and biting into a fiery *wiri-wiri* pepper, he kept thinking...as his tongue burned and his Adam's apple bulged.

Strange, at that moment I imagined people being put into prison in Siberia by Joseph Stalin. Leovski didn't seem like my brother anymore. But he was—my mother insisted.

Auntie, Grandmother – all came around us now.

I again thought about the bus incident when we were children—the chicken fluttering in his hands. Yes, real terror was on his face! Right then Leovski laughed; and he was no longer the revolutionary, and it was just like old times again, if only for our mother's sake.

A sliver of onion stuck out of his left bicuspid; then he muttered something about a large workers' strike looming. My mother's eyes widened. And right after the labour strike, Leovski would announce that he would leave...the Party was sending him away. *Where to?*

My mother grew more anxious.

Leovski didn't jut out his chin Lenin-like this time, and he didn't make any reference to Russian Communism when I tried to nettle him by saying Stalin was the worst dictator the world has known.

Leovski squirmed; he was having second thoughts, maybe about the planned workers' strike. I also dwelled on his harangue about the multinationals not giving back large profits made from the sugar-cane plantation to the local economy; and why did the sugar produced here had to be sent all the way to England to make Cadbury's milk chocolate and exported back to us at a very high price? See, Cadbury's was my favourite!

Leovski used terms like "social infrastructure," and about health and educational development in our country. More statistics he spewed out. But he became glum.

"Hey, Leovski, what's the matter?" I asked.

I addressed him by his real Hindu name, and still he didn't answer. I tried *companero*, pretending to be Castro with a fat cigar hanging from my lips. Then, *tovarish*. And one or two workers called on him to talk about the upcoming labour strike.

What was Leovski really thinking? He murmured something about me being "the Canadian" only. At the next strategy session to plan the upcoming strike, I sat in.

Balram, one of the committed workers, said: "Now's the time to cripple the sugar industry for good. It's a lesson none will ever forget."

"What kind of lesson?" Leovski asked testily.

The workers seemed cowed. But one or two sniggered. Leovski appeared fazed. *Was he really?* A change of thoughts, a change of mind... as more I dwelled upon.

***

For days after Leovski kept to himself, and all my efforts to engage him to defend socialism and communism were to no avail. I tried being testy or argumentative with him, saying socialism was merely a form of dictatorship. Before when I said that he'd rail at me and harangue about the American imperialist system; it was only the democracy of the rich that made millionaires on Wall Street who ran the White House! Capitalism led to imperialism, didn't I know?

"Hey, Leovski, what's the matter now? I'm your brother —tell me!" I almost called him *Comrade*.

He simply shrugged.

"Come on, *Leovski*...what is it?"

113

Then, "That name you call me is only for foreign people," he said glumly.

I looked at how his eyelids quivered.

"The workers...?"

He burst out: "Now what are you, the head of a multinational corporation?"

I waited to hear more.

"I'm going to America!" he let out.

"You...are?"

He lifted his head, chin jutting out. "America... yes."

"What about Russia...Cuba?"

Maybe he'd had a row with the Party bosses; or, he just didn't want to lead another march to take strike action in order to cripple the sugar industry. "The workers – the exploited – they depend on you," I tried coaxing him. "That Balram, for instance..."

"His wife's pregnant again," Leovski moaned.

I asked if he was serious about going abroad to America. And I figured the next day he'd resort to his old self, being the true *revolutionary*. Another bus, *Lord Mountbatten*, passed by on the main road near to where we lived, and the horn blew louder. Then the sugar-cane transport truck named *Zapata* passed by—workers in it hailing as they saw Leovski sitting in our front yard, all in the spirit of true comradeship.

Yet when I called him by his Russian name, he quickly said I shouldn't.

"What are you now?" I didn't want to let him off the hook.

"Che Guevara," he said with a straight face.

"So Che Guevara wants to go to America – to start a revolution?"

He laughed.

The old fire in his eyes again. "Just like you'll be doing in Canada, eh?" he taunted.

"In Canada people have freedom."

"Workers everywhere are exploited!"

"Some people have made it from rags to..." I baited him. Then, "Where in America are the oppressed who will want to join you in overthrowing...?"

"The black people, they're really oppressed," his eyes burned.

Maybe he genuinely wondered about me going to Canada—as much as I wondered about him going to America.

"Where will you get the money from to go to America?" I asked; it was what my mother also wanted to know.

Leovski kept thinking. "Will the Party give you?" I struck out. Another truck lumbered by, more workers hailing him.

"Will *they*?" I pointed to the ones whose faces were smeared with soot from the burnt sugarcane. Then he said: "*You* will give me the money."

His irony didn't escape me.

The truck lumbered down the winding road, a heavy blanket of smoke in its trail. "I will, eh?" I barked.

"You're my brother, no?"

I laughed. He too laughed.

"Look here, Leovski –"

"Don't call me that name anymore!"

"Look here, Che Guevara –"

"Don't call me that either!"

Not by his Hindu name then, which also didn't sound like his name anymore. Ah, maybe I still wanted him to be *Leovski Donov.*

He grimaced.

"The Blacks in America are really the oppressed," he said. "In New York, Chicago, Alabama, Mississippi, in the far south—they need to be liberated." He grew strident as he quoted African-Americans like the Reverend Jessie Jackson. He even quoted du Bois, yes. I'd heard him say some of this into his tape-recorder. My mother quietly listened.

Leovski began telling me how many black people lived in the ghettoes in the inner cities, and the drug addiction, crime, racism, police brutality, and those with HIV/AIDS in America. When I didn't respond, he accused: "Don't you care about them?"

His chin jutted out; and maybe he'd talk about life in Canada next—about the Native peoples, in particular. No, he left that… to me!

"What about the people here, the exploited…?" I asked.

115

He continued on about the blacks in America, how they suffered long decades of slavery in the cotton plantations.

I forced a reply: "So you think *they* will listen to you?"

"Why wouldn't they?"

He continued on about the poor in Toronto, Montreal, Halifax, Vancouver—which really surprised me; and about the police again shooting black people in Canada, not just in Los Angeles.

I expected him to talk next about Native people's plight everywhere, not just in Canada. But he hummed something about not understanding why the Eskimos wanted to live in cold Arctic weather.

I forced a laugh. "They're Canada's first peoples," I said.

He kept thinking about the cold weather in Canada, maybe. Not cold weather in America too, in places like New York? And cold in Siberia...Russia?

My mother looked confused, because she'd never heard of people in America or Canada being poor, or...starving. She'd seen magazine pictures of only well-dressed people, including black people, some who drove in fancy cars. But freezing...in the cold?

My brother looked at me again; he wasn't getting far with me, he knew. Then addressing our mother only, he said: "What are you cooking today?" He was hungry again, as he swallowed emptily.

My mother was glad he was hungry. Surprisingly she said, "In America you will eat as much as you want, eh?" Maybe implying gluttony. She said this too because the situation in our country was going from bad to worse with everyone talking about leaving our shores. And where simple village people got the gumption and money from to make travel arrangements, I didn't know.

Villagers would drop by—workers and peasants –to ask my brother to assist them with spelling their names correctly as they tried applying for a passport and a visa—which he did willingly.

Again I smiled.

***

116

My mother started dishing out food for a hungry Leovski, even as she again wondered if there were indeed poor and homeless people in America. Her eyes narrowed, as a strange fear about America gripped her; and fear also about Canada because of the plight of the Native peoples. A soiled-looking copy of *Granma* on the table I glanced at. My mother's eyes shifted to it, also.

Strange, I seriously began thinking of people in North America doing menial work—in restaurants, hotels, factories—and some planning a long protest march in order to improve their working conditions. Another transport truck painted pink lumbered past—one without a name.

Leovski looked at me; and he knew what I was thinking—about that nameless truck. I imagined it being called *Leovksi Donov.*

"When is he leaving for America?" Balram asked me soon after.

"You mean Comrade Leovski?"

He nodded.

"Is the Party still sending him away?"

Balram was deeply involved in Party work. "He's really one of us, you know." Then he smiled.

I didn't like how he smiled; it was as if he was laughing at my brother seriously thinking of going to America.

I concentrated on Leovski in the kitchen swallowing another mouthful of food, though solemn he looked. "I will remain here," he quietly said, focusing on the plate before him with his favourite fare—rice mixed in with curry sauce.

Right then I saw him being interviewed by a TV crew, as if he was planning a protest march in New York itself; and the announcer was saying: *"Mr Leovski Donov is deeply concerned about the plight of immigrants in these United States of America. Not just the Blacks, the Hispanics, but the illegals, the millions of undocumented immigrants everywhere!"*

A heavy pause.

"So Mr Leovksi Donov," asked the attractive Hispanic female TV interviewer, *"are you yourself an illegal alien?"*

My brother's jutting-out chin; and something about the word *alien* irked him. He looked confused. Then, the picture slowly faded from my mind. I quickly saw him again punctuating the air, gesticulating before a large crowd...as the pink truck lumbered by once more, which the workers had indeed named *Leovski Donov*.

I didn't laugh, though I felt the urge to. But he burst out laughing; he really did—the *revolutionary!*

THE OTHER HALF

Harro felt a stirring in his veins looking at Shami—who was one of our young teachers with jet-black hair, a pointy nose, and a wisp of a body. Harro had lived for a while in America, and might have come back just to meet her. Now friends we were becoming, Harro and I. "What for?" I asked him, and he made a whirring noise. See, his head was a mass of crumpled hair, Afro-style. He was one of our more seasoned teachers, yes. "What for?" he feigned being amused.

I continued thinking about his interest in our East Indian Shami: she being one of the best new teachers recruited from the village. Harro was from the town, different in style and manner. I smiled. Harro made a face, an American face.

Shami whirled her body around as Harro pretended being suave, though he looked ungainly standing near her. When he laughed Shami also laughed. Indeed she knew of his interest in her, older as he was. The senior school kids snickered, as I simply thought of the difference between town and country and what seemed like a new time, or a new era. Maybe it also had to do with the government trying to change people's ways. *Anti-colonialism do you call it?*

Harro kept being charming; and Shami was a Muslim, but not a diehard like her father, Abdul Gafoor. Did Gafoor know about Harro's interest in Shami? Laughter from the other young teachers being aware of the bigotry and diehard religious feelings in our community.

"Why are you watching me like that?" Shami raised her voice to Harro.

"I can watch you if I want," he shot back.

"You think you're still in America, eh?" Shami meant this in a funny way.

"Maybe," Harro grinned.

"It's because you're not like us…village people?" Shami meant to put Harro on the defensive. He passed a hand over his head, smoothing his hair.

She stroked her own hair reaching down to her shoulders.

The other teachers listened in, one or two laughing. I figured our village was a unique place we were committed to. But many of us also set our sights on America. *Yes, going there.* But Harro having returned was making us begin to have second thoughts. Why did he really come back? He would go back to America and never return when the right time came. *But when?*

Shami cast a sideways glance at me, and smiled.

Harro in America in zoot and strutting about in Motown fashion wearing platform shoes with a smirk on his face. In Harlem he was funky-looking. "Hey, Mr American Man," I called out. Harro waved, but waving to Shami only. I saw her leaning against Harro's arm. *Really in America?*

"Why are you grinning like that?" asked Harro.

Who…really?

We watched the older boys play cricket, a favourite school game. Shami walked by looking beautiful as she flaunted herself. Her diehard father, Abdul Gafoor, I again thought about, who regularly prayed at the mosque. Ah, now Shami was beginning to have liberal ideas with our country's schools no longer being run by Christians. "Denominational"—was the government word we repeated to ourselves.

Harro made a strange sound, like an "American" sound.

I imagined Abdul Gafoor talking to the village imam, who recommended that Shami wear a hijab to hide her beauty from the likes of Harro. Shami would look beautiful in a hijab, I knew.

Now some started calling Harro "coloured"–an American term—and he'd said something about having joined the NAACP while in America. I wanted to ask Harro more about this, but he would simply clam up. I wanted him to only talk about America's "coloured" people and their struggle. Shami did too, though she looked at me in a wry manner, pretending she didn't care.

Harro remained cool, American cool. Why did he come back after five long years there? And was Shami really interested in him? "Is it true you're thinking about Harro and maybe going to America?" I teased her.

"No!"

"You can't deny it!"

"Deny what?"

"Harro…and America."

"He's not like us," she made a face. I wanted her to be cool, American-cool. Everyone laughed when I said that. Shami simply dithered.

***

Harro had become disillusioned with America, it seemed, which was the talk going around. Shami came by swaying her smallish body, which she did even when she rode her bicycle going home after school. Harro also rode his bicycle to and from the town to our village. Our village appeared bigger because of the likes of Harro teaching at our school. "America-America," I sang to myself.

New York, Boston, Los Angeles, Atlanta, New Orleans, and Miami came closer. I walked around in my own zoot. Everyone else being in zoot, including the older students. Strutting we were.

121

Our village and country was no longer a dull place. I stood before my class of students with a new confidence. But again others scoffed.

"He go marry she?" one older student sniffed.

"Marry...who?"

"You know who!"

Everything being in a whirl, as my head spun.

"It's because he's...like a white man."

"Who?" I snapped.

"Harro...you know."

I balked. "Not colored...?"

Abdul Gafoor, Shami's father, met with the imam once more. Maybe he didn't want Shami to be a school teacher any longer. But Shami was determined, she would never stop being a teacher. I braced myself for more. Harro, well, only smiled.

"He's really not like us," I heard.

"Because he's...?"

"A Negro," someone hurled.

"Who are we...anyway?" I lit up with an argument.

"Wha...?"

"Harro's mixed-race...white," rasped another.

The wrangle over race continued. I tormented myself thinking about this.

"See, racial problems are everywhere in America, yet everyone wants to go there," Harro smirked, as though having a second thought.

"Why?" I argued, in a vain manner.

Harro's thoughts were only on Shami, he couldn't fool me. When he played cricket with us in the schoolyard, he began to be a show-off—his large body ambling forward as he ran up to bowl. Shami watched him closely as Harro pretended being a fast bowler—like famous Wesley Hall, a much talked-about West Indian player.

Pace like fire, see.

Shami focussed her eyes as Harro once more took the long run-up, then sprang high it seemed as he bowled really fast. I thought of our famous cricketers who travelled the world to England...India, Pakistan, Sri Lanka, Australia. But not to America?

Harro gripped the cricket ball tighter in his hand. He swung his shoulders as he bowled at the batsman. A show-off!

One older student called out to "the American cricketer!" Then, "Come on, let's see how really American you are!" "Yeah-yeah!" Shami applauded. I wasn't sure if she was applauding the village star batsman Munilall...or fast-bowler Harro.

Harro in zoot strutting in Harlem or Motown, then in New York...and next being in Chicago, Los Angeles. I was sitting high up in a large football stadium in New York watching him there in the middle playing cricket. Not baseball! Just then he looked up, he saw me and he waved.

Sauntering down Fifth Avenue in Manhattan next he was, and I was with him. Shami was there, too...her face on the cover of fashion magazines, pointy nose and all. She was really on the cover of *Cosmopolitan,* on newsstands in the Big Apple. *Our Shami!*

Harro looked at these pictures and smiled. When I actually told Shami this, she blushed. She was a Muslim, I mustn't forget. Abdul Gafoor would have none of it. *None of what?* Shami parted her lips, teeth glistening.

Harro was taking Shami's hand again. I told her what I imagined, and how she laughed.

"You must marry me," Harro said to her.

"To take me with you to America?" she grinned; it was just banter.

Abdul Gafoor and the imam grew wide-eyed, as the gossiping grew.

"We could elope," Harro said, being debonair.

"What's elope?" Shami shot back.

Does he mean it?

***

Gafoor was aghast. The imam kept up his solemn face. The muezzin's cry rose at the mosque—calling everyone to prayers.

"Really elope?" Shami repeated.

123

Harro once more did the long run-up with the cricket-ball in his hand. I looked at him closely. "It will never be, Harro, not with Shami's father being who he is," I said to him. And Shami's face still on the cover of *Cosmopolitan*. Then she was on *Reality TV*... and Donald Trump was captivated by her!

The imam frowned. Abdul Gafoor's ire grew.

I said to Harro, "You have to use a different tactic, man."

"What different tactic?"

I didn't want to see him in America, I wanted him to be right here with us. As a young teacher I'd made a commitment to our village and country. Other young teachers were similarly committed, even as we talked about the NAACP, Black Liberation and the Civil Rights Movement in America. Later it would be about saving the environment, the Amazon basin so close to us. America, Canada, Asia, Africa...Saudi Arabia—all came closer.

Shami applauded when the cricket ball flew past the batsman who ducked at the crease! Maybe the school's star batsman, Munilall, had other ideas with Harro bowling at him. Did Munilall want to become a prime minister one day?

"See, Harro, you're not the best," I heckled him.

"I am," he hollered back.

"Harro! Harro!" came a chant.

Chicago, New York, Los Angeles, all chanting. *So cool.*

Harro talked about the Muslims in America, and about Malcolm X, then about Louis Farrakhan. Could Shami's father Abdul Gafoor be such a Muslim? The imam...well, gathered other Muslims around him at the mosque. A minaret sky, the muezzin calling everyone to prayer, if the men only.

***

Shami was nervous when her father came home late that evening. Abdul Gafoor was thinking of sending Shami to another village to be far from Harro.

Shami looked nervous, she simmered.

Gafoor talked about going on the hajj...to Saudi Arabia, devout as he was. Maybe he genuinely feared the "American"

Harro, who read magazines like *Playboy* and wanted to elope with his daughter.

"Tell us about girls in America, Harro?" another teacher baited him.

"You have to go there to see for yourself," he replied.

"To meet Marilyn Monroe, d'you mean?" I tried. Did Harro actually meet her and Elizabeth Taylor? "Is Shami not like her?" I meant Marilyn Monroe, who else?

"Harro's now thinking of becoming a Muslim," another teacher solemnly said.

"No," I replied.

"Abdul Gafoor would accept him if he really became one, eh?" mused another.

"But Harro's, well..." sniffed someone else

"Well what?" I cried. "A Christian?"

Commitment to local politics and tradition is what I really thought about. Did I still want political change? *What kind of change?* I faced the students in my class in the new school term. But my thoughts were only on America; and sometimes about Shami eloping with Harro. But he wouldn't talk about America anymore; Harro only shook his head when I prompted him.

Shami was on his mind, there was no doubt. I saw him and Shami talking animatedly. I rubbed my eyes. Harro was indeed asking her to elope with him! But she was devoted to her father, she wouldn't go with one like Harro.

"You were born here like us, Harro," she tried with her mixed feelings.

"Was I?"

"You only lived a short while in America."

Her words were mine. *What was I thinking?*

"This is not *our* place," Harro shot back.

What did he mean?

Shami walking tall being a real fashion model in America. How she flaunted herself with high heels and walking along Fifth Avenue in New York, then sauntering down Times Square, and on Broadway next. She was also in Los Angeles...San Francisco—with admirers everywhere! Donald Trump was really becoming interested in her. Ah, she would now wear a hijab, looking elegant—if only to defy expectations. *Imagine, eh?*

***

Weeks passed into months. Harro, well, he didn't come to our school anymore; he was teaching elsewhere, it was rumoured. But...not returned to America?

He would teach in a town-school only, but still be interested in our Shami. He would ask no other to *elope* with him. See, I persisted with Shami and Harro being together in America. But other village school teachers scoffed at me.

Abdul Gafoor was like a ghost walking around with his own thoughts. My mind kept becoming haywire. Again I saw Harro taking the long run-up to bowl the cricket ball. I applauded, when no one else did. Harro and Shami walking hand-in-hand in New Orleans' French Quarter.

How the other teachers laughed. Munilall, the star batsman, said I was the only one who would miss Shami because I was secretly in love with her. And Harro would only fall in love with an American beauty, if a genuinely coloured girl like Aretha Franklin. Shami's family members said almost the same, trying to save face. Abdul Gafoor was grim-looking.

I began seeing Harro as a diehard Muslim...going on the hajj with the likes of Louis Farrakhan. Abdul Gafoor would go there, too. I imagined him meeting Harro dressed in a long flowing white robe and looking like a sheik from Oman, Qatar, or Saudi Arabia.

Shami came to our school with her head covered, a devout Muslim. Because of Harro's doing? Everyone said I was becoming strange, or different, in my obsessive thinking about Shami.

Shami's father Abdul Gafoor now wore a long white robe...going on the hajj, and being in Saudi Arabia; so devout he was...bending down, buttocks arched in the air in the *sijdah* and pointing in the direction of the Kaaba. Instinctively he turned sideways and saw Harro next to him—as they made eye-contact, praying hard.

PART THREE

JAGNATH & TOMBY

All is race, there is no other truth.

—Disraeli

A new government and a new people were in power, and Tomby steeled himself for more to come as his mind went back and forth to the trinity-peaked mountain-range island of his birth. Now in his twilight years—a retiree from academia–he felt the urge to "give something back." *But give what back?* Charles looked at his friend sitting across from him in the Indian restaurant with an uncanny feeling in his mind. They would talk frankly about the importance of seeing the region—meaning the Caribbean—objectively, now that they lived abroad and being in the *diaspora:* the latter itself an amorphous term.

Tomby deliberated on what would be an ideal government for the region as a whole. Surf beating on a far shore; and living in Ottawa he'd started to feel he no longer *belonged*, which he dwelled upon sometimes until the early hours of the morning—

here in Canada's capital city and the seat of the federal government. Charles, a retired civil servant, simply nodded indulgently to his friend.

Tomby recalled the arm-chair Faculty Club meetings he attended where his professorial colleagues reminisced about some of their past students, and the publish-or-perish syndrome, and the newest jargon in academia called *post-modernitis*, like a strange disease. He yawned reflexively; he must see his doctor again if only to hear about a prostate gland "problem." Charles hummed about a weak aorta valve in his heart, a hoax put on him by the Maker.

Tomby laughed.

Charles also laughed.

Stronger waves beating in the Caribbean Sea. Tomby dwelled on the new people literally taking over the island. *Indians at the helm, see.* Charles grunted, but seemed amused by what kept sending Tomby "back there". And their wives, Dora and Hyacinth, got on really well, let it be known. Charles lamented that he'd worked in the government far too long as Dora, his wife, often teased him about. Tomby blithely reacted to his own wife's qualms about him living only the academic life and removed from *real* people; and yes, he now saw himself as "a creative consultant." He also mused about his prostate gland problem, and his French-Canadian medic, Dr. Fleury, told him to get more exercise. *Get on the treadmill. Listen to what your tubes tell you!*

Island-waves beating; and everything, or everyone, seemed tied to racial heritage, like a strange fate they shared, thought Tomby.

Damn, race! Charles simply glanced round the Indian restaurant as if looking for a familiar face as he swallowed the tasty chicken vindaloo.

Tomby recalled stories about when the former island-prime minster, Dr Grantley—the bespectacled one—held the reins of government and didn't pander to people's whims after the island gained independence from Britain. Tomby figured they didn't make them like Dr Grantley anymore—whose intellect mixed with oratory made him spell-binding. Charisma, yes.

Charles suggested that while it might have been a suitable black government then, things often got out of hand when crime soared. Tomby made a face. Random acts of violence had become an everyday occurrence tied to drug-trafficking. *Who else saw it?* And Indian young women were really kidnapped because they came from rich families. Let the calypsonians sing about it. Chutney and soca, ah. The carnival-men beating pan with Bad-Johns being everywhere!

Tomby saw the urgent need for honesty and transparency in government all over the Third World. The political scientist in him, yes. Charles, a regular church-goer, nodded; and he hoped to write a novel one day. "I've always had literary interests," he said.

"Really?" A smile flitted across Tomby's mahogany-coloured face.

"Being in the government didn't give one much time to do creative writing," Charles complained.

"I remember how back on the island you were keen on drama."

"You too, man."

"Now writing a novel, is it?"

Charles moaned about the novel's changing form, and about plot as he knew it being no longer important in the post-modernism craze going around. The novel must only mirror life. And it was all due to the influence of Virginia Woof and James Joyce—that stream-of-consciousness literary crowd.

Tomby looked at Charles in some surprise. Charles added that he was slowly coming to grips with the complexity of the narrative form. Lips tightened, facial muscles pulsed. Tomby looked disinterestedly at his friend. "You must no longer have real plot, is that it?" he asked.

Charles shot back, "Man, we're a Caribbean people, we like plots."

"Like our calypso has plots?"

"It's narrative form we're talking about."

"Destiny, too," Tomby rasped.

Really that?

Tomby was thinking of writing his own book about governance with his socialist ideas embedded in it. A book he would no doubt self-publish if no academic press was interested in it. Charles muttered something about the novel being the best literary form to make one's point of view heard, more than what any government bureaucrat hoped to write.

"You want to outdo VS Naipaul, is that it?" remarked Tomby with a slight grin.

"Yes, er, no," Charles shook his head.

They'd previously talked about Naipaul, or *Nye-Powell*, and how the island's intellectuals growled about his manner, ethnicity commingling with poetics. And the resentment or animosity that seemed to exist between Derek Walcott and V.S. Naipaul in the Caribbean, and the bantering about them at soirees where men with their attractively-coiffed wives swallowed deep-fried prawns and bemoaned the spat between the two literary giants.

Ribald laughter followed about who was the "The Mongoose".

Charles moaned that writing a novel was really taxing work. So many drafts had to be done, and one's distinctive voice must be heard as the novel slowly took shape and form. Tomby averred something about "effective multiculturalism" in governance, and writing a book focussing on existentialism tied to "the orgasm of life," as he called it.

Really that?

Roots, culture and folklore being a new form of syncretism more than what the academic historians could unearth from the archives.

Imagine their wives laughing their hearts out. Oh, women always did. Then it was back to their African forebears. But not forebears also from India and China…and Europe? The English, French, Spanish and Dutch all being in the picture. *Creole, d'you know?*

Tomby was beguiling in his manner. Charles lit up with more argument about narrative form. Tomby simply reminisced about when he was a kid living close to the town of Chaguanas (a name mimicked on the island), and his best friend was the East Indian boy, Jagnath.

Go on, tell me more.

132

Poor then Tomby's family was...when he'd lived with Grandma Edna; and he'd kept hanging around the Jagnath household, a wealthy business family. Sea-breezes all around...as he and Jagnath traipsed around the village in their carefree schoolboy days.

"Here we're like brothers," Jagnath sang.

"Are we?" asked Tomby with laughter.

Jagnath grabbed his African friend's hand, digging into his flesh.

Ouch! Play-acting...the boys' arms linked. But Jagnath's father had other ideas; he who owned two trucks with which he transported goods from one place to another with a sense of his Hindu beliefs uppermost, for he named one truck *Shiva*, and the other *Vishnu*. Did he look askance at his son Jagnath mixing with Tomby?

Tomby was African, make no mistake about it; and his grandmother was a devoted Baptist. In the background somewhere... African slavery relived, like regular island pastime.

"Not India, too?" asked Jagnath.

Tomby simply laughed back.

Grandma Edna, rheumy-eyed, with a Bible in hand and a hymn-book at her side, nodded her head.

Here now in the Ottawa restaurant Tomby listened to his friend Charles talk more earnestly about narrative technique, and memory was the Mother of the Muses. Tomby harrumphed. Oh yes, islanders like themselves who lived too long abroad, and would only reminisce like regular pastime.

Tomby added that he simply wanted to face up to the challenge that St. Margarita presented. The restaurant they were in named *Sitar* with aromatic smells from the culinary spices rose around them. Their eyes shifted to the authentic décor depicting the many Indian deities.

Tomby admitted that the vindaloo was the best curry he'd ever tasted. And why couldn't black people's food be as tasty?

Let the wives laugh all they wanted. Now who first grew rice in the Caribbean but slaves, though Indians claimed they were first? Charles swallowed another mouthful of tasty chicken and Basmati rice. *Blessed Indians!*

Tomby thought it was a miracle that he'd been able to attend university after he achieved an island scholarship. But his friend Jagnath wasn't so lucky because Jagnath's father didn't have the right "connection". Maybe Dr Grantley turned away from an entire race of people on the island with his Black Power instincts at work. And Jagnath senior wanted his son to become a *pandit* and uphold the Hindu tradition, though they were far from India.

Jagnath would be surprised to see him now, Tomby thought.

He'd go back to the island from time to time to meet relatives, though Grandma Edna had passed on; but he'd never bothered to look up Jagnath. Charles looked at his friend in puzzlement.

Plot, you see.

Now it was the East-Indian people's turn in government. Tomby simply reverted to that time on the island when the British *governed* and everything seemed to be in harmony. Again he recalled how he and Jagnath would frolic around and climb jamoon and guava trees and fish to their hearts' content for cascadoux and crabs.

"Tomby, is all we goin to get t'day?" Jagnath called out about their catch.

"You sure, Jag?"

"Let's go fo it!"

Billows, the tide rising with the Caribbean Sea and the Atlantic Ocean. And the two boys kept having the best time of their lives. The trucks lumbered by with the deities' names blared out. But how threatened was the Jagnath family about Black Power on the island?

Muslim extremism, also, with an emblazoned X written after some firebrand's name! Charles shook his head, with plot still being all.

Tomby forced a grin.

Charles swallowed more bean curd. Tomby murmured about *jelabi* being his favourite Indian dessert. And did St. Margarita now have a prime minister with a distinct name...*Kamala?* The word *kama* resonated, a derivative meaning goddess of love—a symbolic reference point.

Tomby wiped his lips with a soiled napkin; he hummed something about a new economic theory as he invoked Nobel Prize-winning economist Gary Becker's *homo economicus* that "more is better". Now, too, there was talk of the Emotional Economy, what the likes of Adam Smith never considered. Capitalism on the march! Whither socialism?

On the island news was still about rape increasing with 260 incidents reported in one year compared to 365 last year. Charles had a sombre face. And the new female prime minister was taking control of the situation—as the media reported—determined to bring an end to crime by calling in help from Scotland Yard.

Tomby let out a distinct moan. Jagnath was now an ethnic-Indian politician chomping at the bits with the new party's slogan. Prime Minister Kamla Devi-Bihar going overseas to proclaim her government, if only to burnish her island's image...thinking it wasn't just a crime-ridden place as she told large crowds of émigrés in New York, South Florida, Toronto. The media followed her wherever she went.

Tomby kept thinking about governance. "Kamala Devi, who's she really?" he asked almost rhetorically.

"How real d'you mean?" Charles shot back.

"Kama...not karma."

The new prime minister would be speaking at Harvard University next. Tomby nodded gravely. Jagnath being in the prime minister's entourage dressed in authentic Indian garb and talking about the newest Hindu deity. Charles sighed. *Real plot, you see.*

Hyacinth and Dora, their wives, were in solidarity with Kamala Devi-Bihar, because of women's power was now at the fore. It didn't matter what race she was from. Follow the example of Jamaica's female prime minster!

"No-no," Charles cackled.

Tomby felt strangely irritated.

Once more Charles muttered something about the novel's changing form. *Plot...murder!* Narrative, you see.

***

"You want to write the best Caribbean novel, is that it?" asked Tomby pointedly. "Still wrestling with it?"

"Oh, wrestling…indeed," Charles yawned.

"Why not write the best Canadian novel then? You've been living here long enough in North America, man. Canada's more than just an imaginary place."

Charles made a face. "It's the best damned Caribbean novel I only want to write," he forced the words out.

"Better than Naipaul wrote?"

"With plot, see."

"Ah, murder!"

Knives and forks clinked in the restaurant run by a Bengali family—people who'd moved around after Partition in India.

"Murder indeed," Charles echoed.

And was Prime Minister Kamala Devi-Bihar's life in danger? Tomby looked dourly at his friend Charles. Jagnath, where was he going next with the Prime Minister's travelling entourage?

Charles tried figuring out what form his novel must actually take. Not what the new government in St. Margarita would look like as a Caribbean model state…with Tomby looking at him. *Whose Caribbean are we now talking about?* The restaurant manager started picking up plates, cutlery.

Tomby and Charles agreed that narrative form without concocting violence would be implausible. Yes, a new crime wave was in the making. And the novel's closure must be contemplated far more than an aesthetic exercise.

The restaurant-owner looked at the twosome with a jaundiced eye.

A perfect ending was what mattered most in fiction, Charles again yawned. Tomby muttered about having eaten too much vindaloo—what he would never tell his doctor about; and right then he wished his friend Jagnath was close by, and for them, well, to taste some genuine cascadura fish-curry.

Tomby belched and looked back at the restaurant owner nodding to them at the doorway. Charles began drifting away…soon to be out of sight. St. Margarita…or Canada…with new governance in the making, Tomby ruminated.

Charles distantly waved back to his friend. The wives also waved, even as they kept contemplating women's special place in history—like genuine narrative without a contrived ending. Wind and waves and surf beating...more than symbolically; and indeed, good governance was what everyone should become aware of, nothing more compelling. *Murder foretold!*

BLACK LIKE WHO?

He'd be meeting Esmeralda again to renew their friendship and a smile flitted across Harish's thin mouth. He reminisced on how they'd often berate the other employees when they worked together in the government. Esmee would laugh when one male work colleague literally *ran* to the machine making xerox copies in order to give the impression of being so busy. *Yes, why not?* Esmee's face flitted in and out of his mind. And preparing ministerial briefing notes was what they were good at—"Q's and A's" for *Question Period* in Parliament. They'd also processed the many ethnic groups' applications for funding in the Multiculturalism Unit—the "interest groups," as the media often called them. Esmee would sneer:

"How much more ethnic can we get?"

"How much more?" Harish chuckled.

He'd left the government a full year now. Odd, he felt he was in a wilderness of sorts; the high-tech company he worked for no longer satisfied him. And Esmee (Esmeralda) was still in her government office going through ethnic files and reviewing applications for funding. "Makes me feel like I want to go back to the Caribbean," she'd said to him. "Don't you wish the same, Harish?"

Go...really where?

To India with the sense of *Hindutva*, meaning India for Hindus. His parents back in Gujarat being at it, yes. "It's not just about the monsoon, is it?" Esmee had teased him. When Monique, a French-Canadian work colleague, had said that it would take two or three generations for new immigrants to become *real* Canadians Esmee quickly scoffed at her.

Harish sniffed, *Christ!*

"Look, we're in this together—as Canadians, I mean," Esmee grated.

"No-one can take that away from us," Harish replied.

Take what away?

Esmee's eyes lit up; and Jamaican-born she was; but a new breed of Canadian womanhood was in the making. Harish simply nodded. And laughter, as they mocked how ethnic-group leaders would phone the Minister's office to complain if their funding applications had been turned down. *Cheeky bastards!* Did Black groups get more funding because they were the most discriminated against? Who are *visible minorities* anyway?

And who said what about "the ethnic vote"? Ever heard of a Charter of Values and the fear and controversy of hejab-wearing Muslim women in Quebec? "It's not *multiculturalism* any longer?" railed one white male co-worker in his constant busyness.

"Women's empowerment it is now," sang Esmee, like a non sequitur.

"Yeah."

Harish looked forward to meeting Esmee again after the year seemed to have gone by so quickly. She might even tell him what had actually *changed* in government. "Harish, nothing ever really changes," she would likely reply.

"Our special lunches together, remember?"

"We're privileged in a way, Harish."

139

Newcomers steadily landing at the Pearson International Airport. "Are you Jamaican, not Trinidadian?" Then, "You're not an economic refugee, are you?"

"I'm not from Uganda, sir."

"Chased out by Idi Amin?"

"No, er...that again."

The media blared it out about another boatload of illegal migrants from Fuzhou Province organized by Big Sister Pinge landing on Canadian shore! And those from Yugoslavia, Romania, Syria and the Middle East yet coming. *Somewhere a terrorist threat?*

Harish would cynically remind Esmee about Anglo-Brian's love-interest in her. "God, he's not my type!" she snapped. *Who's really her type?*

Harish had confided to Esmee that he wanted to leave the government. "What for?" she cried. "It's not, well, fulfilling work," he answered.

"You will be losing power," she threw at him. *What power?*

Wasn't Canada really a social experiment on how to "accommodate diversity"? "The department will now appoint the *blackest* person to head the Division," snickered one work colleague.

"Not woman's empowerment then?"

"Don't throw that at me, Harish."

Esmee called him "Asian." Who...or what was *Asian?* And the words from Ann Frank's diary on the poster he'd mounted in his office came back to him. Now hate crimes in Prince George, B.C., and about growing anti-Semitism. Esmee's face her darkish-red lips and pearly white teeth. And the new director to be appointed in the Department who would likely be the "blackest man around"?

"He's a blasted Anglo-Blackson," Esmee grated a reply.

"Oh?"

"We're all ethnics together."

Did Harish not feel a special loyalty to Asians? His mother in Gujarat on the phone asking when he would get married. *Not a love-match for him?* "It must be one like us, Son," urged his mother. "She will be a visible minority, Mommiji," he'd replied.

What are you saying, she will not be Indian like us?"

"Well…"

"We've been making arrangements, Harish, for a girl from a good family. Convent-educated, with good earning power. Your father will study the astrological chart if you provide the date of birth of this one you're seeing." Pause. "Is this girl a… *Canadian?*"

"She's dusky-looking, Mommiji."

"Dusky…what's her name?"

"Esmee."

"Who's this Esmee, eh?"

"She's from the Caribbean."

"Not Canada then?"

"She is, Mommiji."

"Where's she born? This *Caribbean*…is it a province of Canada?"

Harish mimicked his mother as he related this conversation to Esmee, with laughter.

"Is she not like us then, this Esmee?" his mother had raised her voice. "She's, well…black," he shot back an answer.

"Not wheaty, like Canadian girls?"

Harish stifled a yawn.

"Will she bend down and touch my feet to show respect, you tell me? Now this Canada, what kind of place is it becoming?"

"Just like India…with many races and religions living side by side, multicultural—all one country."

"Never mind the Muslims and Partition; it's all that Jinnah's fault!"

"You don't understand life in Canada…"

"How I will live with my grandchildren who speak African only?"

Esmee again laughed teasing him about it. *Now what if…?* Imagine Esmee going with him on a tourist trip to the subcontinent: first to Mumbai, the gateway to the East and walking arm-in-arm. The loafer on the sidewalk charming a cobra looking up at…*them!* And at the fabulous Taj Mahal Hotel they would stay in as "Canadians," then visit a Bollywood film-set.

Imagine Esmee becoming a Bollywood movie-star playing alongside Shah Rukh Khan. But Esmee might be outraged by the slums she would see far from South Mumbai? *She's a Canadian, remember.* Try talking to Esmee about spirituality in India—Not Hindutva anymore? Finally he would take Esmee to meet his mother.

Bapre bap! His mother coming face-to-face with Harish's bride-to-be! Relatives and friends were bowled over by Esmee's confident manner—she definitely wasn't like those from Somalia or Ethiopia who came to study in India.

Esmee's turn: taking Harish to the Caribbean, and lolling around on a sandy beach in bright sunshine. And they would eat akee and salted cod cooked with pimento together. See, he felt "accepted"— the way he never did in Canada.

Oh, tell.

***

Harish braced himself for it—meeting Esmee again, and sure, they'd relive some of the past and maybe compare notes about differences in the public and private domains now that he worked for a private company. "We must meet soon," Esmee urged him on the phone.

"Yes-yes." Harish had really requested a "business" meeting after all, for he'd been hired as a consultant by the high-tech company to promote "cultural diversity" programming. He offered himself as an "expert" in race relations and in order to implement a genuine "cultural-sensitivity awareness" program for the company.

"I'm available to meet you at 2 o'clock," Esmee had replied.

Words Harish played back in his mind. "I will be on time, Esmee." Strange, the words from Ann Frank's diary mounted in his former office came back to him. Harish went up the elevator of the government office building in Gatineau, the Quebec side next to Ottawa. He immediately sensed "power" in the air.

Self-consciously Harish flicked the lapel of his blazer and pulled his tie straight—he, with his *Asian* good looks?

Monique rushed past him, hurrying to the xerox machine. The new associate deputy minister was promoting a "positive employment strategy". Harish confidently walked to his once-familiar office area, hoping to boast to Esmee the details of a business plan he drummed up—an "organizational plan" to commemorate March 21, the UN International Day for the Elimination of Racial Discrimination which the government promoted.

Would Esmee evaluate "his" organizational plan in order to assess it for its African-Canadian content? Harish nodded to a "wheaty Canadian" sitting in the office he once occupied. She smiled back at him.

Esmee wasn't in her office, though she expected him to be on time. The wheaty woman in the next-door office kept up a friendly smile. Harish's gaze languidly drifted to the many files on Esmee's desk. "Esmee would be here soon," he heard again. Another fifteen minutes went by.

Was Esmee deliberately keeping him waiting? *Woman's power!*

Harish unconsciously conjured up his mother in Gujarat yet asking when he would get married. "Is it to someone from Colombia...Ecuador?" Her voice trailed off.

"No, Mommiji!"

"Then, who...a refugee?"

Harish stole a glance at Esmee's appointment book after half-an-hour had gone by. He saw Esmee coming down the corridor with her head up in the air. "Nice to see you, Mr Harish." She didn't apologize for keeping him waiting.

"Yes, nice," he replied. Unconsciously he flicked at his dark blazer.

Something about a Department women's meeting she'd been attending. Esmee's professional air...Instinctively Harish felt his jacket wasn't dark enough.

Esmee asked about the company he represented, in a monotone. And, "How does your organization intend to eradicate racism?" Tell her about "cultivating respect," buzz words that came to him easily, and about "civic participation," "social equality," and "identity". *Christ, why doesn't she apologize for being almost an hour late?*

143

Mr Johnson, the Anglo-Blackson director, approached. Esmee quickly got up...after only a few minutes meeting with Harish. The wheaty woman who occupied his former office grinned.

Esmee picked up the file on top of the heap on her desk. "Goodbye," Harish heard—as Esmee sauntered off to meet the director.

Harish walked back to the elevator, but not before turning around to see Mr Johnson's arm extended to Esmee's shoulder. *Mentoring?* The wheaty girl waved. The xerox machine kept humming. The elevator moved up and down. The poster on the wall of his former office he'd put up a year ago came back to him, the words Harish often mulled over...from Ann Frank's diary he mumbled to himself: *"In spite of everything, I still have faith in human beings."*

Caribbean waves beating, then crashing down... far from Arabian Sea. His mother's voice on the phone once more. "Yes, Mommiji," Harish replied. *"In spite of everything...."* he murmured to himself—taking a longer stride, thinking about a far place, and where else to go.

THE GOOD, THE BAD, AND THE HOOGHLY

(One)

Mathematical models with equations literally hummed in his mind. Incessant, nagging. His theory about how humans walk, their gait being methodical with the legs moving forward in a constant rhythm, Dr Aziz said. His eye-movements, I followed. "You could really tell a lot by someone's walking motion"; and he refused the prefix "Doctor" to his name. "What's a PhD anyway? A professor is just a _processor_ of information." Then it was about how blood flows through the arteries as Aziz quoted Thomas Harvey about the heart's mechanism. "Everything boils down to a mathematical formula," he added.

"Are you sure?"

"Sure?" He shrugged his slight sixty-nine-year-old frame. The Rideau River's water flowed, the current wavering before us; and next it'd be about how far he was from Calcutta and the Hooghly River. He regaled me how as a boy of eleven he'd been devoted to his Hindu teacher who encouraged his class to dwell on what's constantly in motion. *Think about it!*

"It's about physical properties," the teacher said, throwing chalk up in the air:

Up and down.
Up-down.

The chalk thrown sideways next, as the teacher asked his pupils to measure the velocity and the trajectory, and tell how long it took for it to come down. "Gravity," Aziz intoned. Ah, young Aziz–a skinny runt—loved his Hindu teacher more than his Muslim parents; and to Bhola Babu, the teacher, it didn't matter if Aziz was a Muslim or Hindu.

Years later when Aziz returned home from his studies abroad long after Partition with Muslims and Hindus gone their separate ways, he went to see his old teacher in East Pakistan. He found Bhola Babu in a water-logged village close to the Sundarbans.

Up-down, Aziz greeted him.

"Acha, bhai," the teacher replied, "I remember you."

Dr Aziz went down on his knees and touched the old man's feet: *pranam,* with his Canadian degrees hanging from his shirt-sleeves; and it didn't matter if the teacher had a lowly Indian BA; for Aziz it was what was constantly in motion.

Now did I consider the trajectory of my own life? Aziz began telling me more about how when he'd studied in England and his English landlady insisted that he came from India only, not East Pakistan. Aziz countered that he was indeed from Pakistan.

"You're from India," she scoffed.

"The English have their set ways," Aziz finally said to me, shaking his head.

"Pakistan is India too," the landlady rebuked. She'd followed Gandhi's career, for the Mahatma had gripped ordinary English people's lives, especially the flinty English women working in factories with his spiritual force. "Yes, fair-minded the women were," Aziz concluded.

"Fair-minded," I echoed.

The same landlady, upon seeing him when he'd come down for breakfast without his tie, chided: "Look here, I don't want to see you naked." "I'm not a naked fakir," he retorted. See, he wasn't a Bengali without pride.

He vividly remembered growing up in old Calcutta; and with a friend from his village in Solalanpur, in Khulna district, he'd gone on a jaunt in the big city. "Calcutta was beautiful then, the way the British kept it, like another London in the East: the streets, the Howrah train station, the Hooghly River—not like how it is today." Aziz moaned, fingering the large-framed glasses plump on his nose. His neighbours in the district outside Calcutta were Hindus, and his Hindu teacher, Bhola Babu, had invited him to spend the night with his family. "So much he liked me, this schoolmaster," said Aziz.

But he'd peed on his bed. *It was his greatest shame.*

"Bhola Babu never scolded me. From then in I began seeing mathematical models everywhere," Aziz reminisced.

"It's the kind of engineering I wanted to do in Canada. I've attended conferences all over the world, the last time in Vietnam," he went on. But his thoughts drifted back to Bengal— to when Gandhi had been assassinated; and to the time of poet Rabindranath Tagore's passing. "We knew something important happened on the day Tagore died; everyone became so silent." I must know about other writers too during that period, Aziz said—like Bankim Chandra Chatterjee.

"But no one knows Bankim Chandra in the west, do they?" he rasped...since I called myself an English teacher. "Maybe not," I replied.

Not only know Vikram Seth, he scolded, for I'd mentioned the name of the popular Indian author who'd come to Canada. "He's not like Bankim Chandra," Aziz rebuked. Then, "So much they miss out these days, these students. Have they ever read *The Night-Owl's Sketches?*"

Flies flitted around us in the park. Aziz coughed lightly, he'd swallowed a fly...like a new trajectory.

Up-down!

I pictured him before his class at the local university where he was a mathematics professor. With chalk in hand symbols, equations, quickly formed, and it was quantum this-or-that.

Aziz talked to me about his first marriage, an arranged affair. Did he expect unhappiness in his life, what no abstract mathematical theory could have predicted? "There's a natural balance in the universe affecting marriages," he said, for everything has a certain "carrying capacity"; it was more than a perpendicular-this, or a circumference-that.

I looked at him with a strange awe. And an aversion for India slowly developed in his mind because of his ingrained Muslim identity, Aziz said. Yes, he'd enjoyed it when the Japanese attacked India during World War Two. "The excitement of war, bombs, and planes. We were young then." And Aziz couldn't get the British out of his mind with their tramcar system running so efficiently.

His thoughts drifted to the time when he'd been asked to give a keynote speech in Philadelphia on "Uncertain Parabolic Systems: A Games Problem." As he addressed his audience, he immediately saw different pathways everywhere coming to him like an epiphany. Aziz talked on about the difference between temperate and tropical peoples, different social behavior patterns, almost like a parabolic system. "Back there"—he meant Bangladesh—"everyone talks to people about their problems, sharing information, but not here." He paused, allowing this to sink in.

Did I share this belief?

"Here in the west people go to a therapist to help them," Aziz berated me. "Now you hear so much about PTSD."

I nodded.

Then it was about his second marriage which failed–his first wife had died young—and everyone advised him to go and see a psychiatrist. "But the therapist only repeated what's written in his book *Coping with a Bad Marriage*," Aziz ridiculed.

"About cognitive–" I tried.

"Cognitive behavior bullshit?" he railed.

He went on about probability factors and people thinking they're so clever when they are not. "Now wars are fought everywhere," he said. "Arabs fighting Arabs, and Muslims with their Sharia law and what's Hadith, eh? Just the Prophet's sayings." And about marriage: was it really the union of souls?

He intimated about nightmares he'd been having: images of blackness, and the river being so black, and the clouds black-black.

Aziz resorted to solving mathematical problems as his way to fly over the *blackness*. "I'm literally flying 40 miles above the earth, and it's only differential dynamics." But the dark dreams kept returning.

Back to the image of his first wife, Tabitha: how she'd held up his books for him when he worked on mathematical problems. "But she died young from a strange illness," Aziz lamented. His second marriage came soon after—also an arranged affair—but this new wife was the sullen type. Aziz grew bitter. He resorted to mathematics. He turned to look at the Rideau River before us, everything moving with its own volatility. "It's because of what I keep dreaming," he suggested. A wistful gaze entered his eyes. He looked away, far away.

(Two)

Recall: the Conference in Philadelphia he'd attended where he talked about thermodynamics. But Dr Aziz encountered a European-looking woman with a shaven head in a Philly side street who wore a flowing saffron-coloured robe with filigree around her neck. Making eye-contact with him, she said she'd just gotten off the *Mayflower*, and was bent on finding God in the New World.

Why? Aziz asked her.

"You're Hindu, you should know about God. Tell me what am I doing here in America?" she said.

Aziz's thoughts flitted back to his old teacher, Bhola Babu: about Hindus being an intellectual people, not just holy men, as he told the Philly woman. He remembered how his old teacher in those days would use words with such eloquence: "The speeches of Winston Churchill, he read them to us and you'd think he was Churchill himself. And Jules Verne's *Journey to the Centre of the Earth*—Bhola Babu brought up scenario after scenario," boasted Aziz.

"But aren't Muslims an intellectual people too?" I asked.

He heaved in, thinking...*what?* About the once-great Ottoman Empire; and how Muslim people in the West were now discriminated against. "From the time of the Mughals, the Hindus started conniving with the British, the maharajahs' only purpose being to overthrow the Mughals." Intellectual...not conniving? The same he told the Philly Hare Krishna woman. And, everything must have an empirical formula. "What is minus infinity plus infinity?" he challenged me to know.

I balked.

He urged the Philly woman to contemplate on a different matrix in her life. *Transcendental reality.*

Aziz had stopped believing in God. Then he talked about his son whom he loved more than anyone else—a boy he named after a US basketball player. But his son pestered him: "How far away are the stars, Dad?"

"How far away?" Aziz shot back.

"Dad, you heard me."

"Many light years away, Michael."

"How do you... well, measure it?"

"See, 186,000 miles per second light travels. Now calculate it, 186,000 times 60 seconds x 60 minutes x 24 hrs x 365 days a year..."

Michael sighed wearily. Aziz figured he was slowly becoming estranged from his son, for the boy was living with his mother—whom Aziz called "the witch". *Why?* Michael wanted to know.

Why what? Aziz grimaced.

And two elderly Bengali men he'd met in his walkabout in the park with whom he had heated discussions about God: one Hindu, the other Muslim. The former did yoga exercises; the other was from Bangladesh and had lived in London, but couldn't fit in with the British-Bangladeshi crowd. To both men Aziz declared that God didn't exist. The elderly men's faces became ashen!

Aziz's dark dreams returned. And the Muslim-Bangladeshi man believed Osama bin Ladin was still alive; and the Hindu kept thinking about going back to Benares and bathe in the Ganges River.

Up...down!

The two Bengali men didn't believe in evolution either–for why did apes suddenly stop evolving? *Really...why?* The men would bring their wives to the park; but the Muslim man's wife never looked at any male in the eye for it was forbidden by Sharia law. The Hindu man's wife meditated on Brahma as she recalled an accident in a Mumbai side street when a rickshaw had nearly knocked her over. *Bapre bap!*

Aziz repeated to them that God didn't exist. But the Muslim man told him that his name–*al Aziz*–is one of Allah's ninety-nine names; it means "the Exalted and the Almighty"; and did the name suit him?

Aziz was only devoted to what was abstract. "Mathematics... and sex," he blithely said—what an Italian professor once told him: that one's biological needs always come first, then mathematics.

"It's the way of the world," Aziz hummed. "Maybe it's the same President Bill Clinton experienced with Monica Lewinsky." I looked at him with unease. "No?" he grimaced.

When a female student had sat in the front row in his class with her mini-skirt pulled up, he quickly told her to go and sit at the back—for only then could he concentrate on mathematics. Later that evening a picture of his first wife, Tabitha, reappeared. Aziz's wry conclusion: "Canadian women are beautiful, but they have hard hearts."

Back to his son, Michael, as Aziz dolefully said: "Maybe I won't see him again. Michael dislikes mathematics; he's only interested in politics; he wants to be like Barack Obama. "What for?" Aziz asked him. "Why not?" Michael shot back.

Aziz quoted Tagore to me: "Something undreamt of was lurking everywhere, and every day the uppermost question was where, oh where, would I come across it?" A farther distance, tied to a new matrix. I simply heaved in.

(Three)

The human race—it was all sound and fury, signifying nothing: as Aziz quoted Shakespeare's *Macbeth*. Then, "Are we happier as a human race though we have progressed?" He dwelled on the difference between Western and Eastern culture. "In Bangladesh you quickly know people's thoughts, unlike how it is here," Aziz said. And the best time in his life was when he would spring from tree to tree in Bengal. "As a child it was so special, the freedom."

I nodded.

He talked on about his native language, Bengali, which has 30 letters in the alphabet, and about members of the family having distinct words like *chachi...chacha,* so musical-sounding. And about the Hooghly River and the silt coming down into it from the Himalayas. "Everything grows in Bangladesh, you just put seed into the soil and a plant appears. Look at the Sundarbans."

Once more he quoted Macbeth to me. When a Jewish English professor walked by us in the park, Aziz accosted him: "What does Shakespeare mean by a tale told by an idiot?" The professor fled. Back to his former teacher, Bhola Babu: "You should hear him recite Shakespeare, there was none like him, Latif," Aziz said to me.

His greatest regret was about his children. "They don't even want to put flowers on their mother's grave, my first wife's. Maybe I'm just a sentimental old man." He again invoked Rabindranath Tagore, who was a rich man, but despite that he was a good poet. Next to Tagore, Bankim Chandra Chatterjee was the best. "*Read him,*" Aziz insisted. He'd contemplated writing a book about human nature—"The Mathematical Model of the Mind: Measures of Human Fragility and Consciousness."

Really that.

"Oh, I'm just a mathematician," Aziz moaned, then casually recited lines from *Punch* magazine:

Have you read the Poison Tree
of Bankim Chandra Chatterjee?

We drifted along the park where we saw a man sitting with his legs folded, Buddha-style, eyes closed. Unconsciously I made a scoffing noise. "Respect him," Aziz said to me, sotto voce. *Must I?* Again he quoted Shakespeare. Then he recalled what a government scientist had recently said to him—that life's greatest satisfaction was having sex. "Can you believe that?"

"Helter skelter," I replied nonchalantly.

"Who are you now...Charles Manson?"

'Sex, drugs, and rock an' roll,*"* I mocked, invoking Mick Jagger of the *Rolling Stones.*

Aziz talked on about his all-time favourite movies—*Samson and Delila* and *The Ten Commandments.* "Not *Lawrence of Arabia?"* I challenged him. "What are you, an Arab?"

"An Englishman," I mocked.

Then it was what he'd recently told a Mexican graduate student. "Why be so obsessed with mathematics?"

"Why not?" Hidalgo shot back.

"Try to enjoy life."

Yes, all sound and fury.

(Four)

His dark dreams came back, and an image of a great path opening up before him, because Aziz resorted to always thinking about his first wife, Tabitha, who in the Mathematics Department they called *exotic.* And the doctors had made him sign many forms when she was in the intensive-care unit during her critical illness. "Every doctor was on vacation when my wife died...alone," Aziz remembered—and what a Bangladesh doctor had told him: "Always try to be close to your wife...." Words he never forgot.

When he went past a graveyard, he would wait there for a moment, then walk by. He imagined then that when there's a cyclone or monsoon the rain represented rebirth, and the clouds in one's dreams signify a balance between analytical thought and one's touchy-feely emotions. Tagore's words once more: "Grow like a summer flower, magnificently; die like an autumn leaf, quietly and beautifully."

Aziz muttered, "Mathematically we know the world will end. The galaxies, the planets... and 40 miles from Earth, it's dark matter." He railed, "Cyclones, why can't scientists stop cyclones? Temperature and currents come from the ocean, and a tsunami... so much happening we really don't know much about." His face crinkled into a strange smile.

An attractive woman walked by us—the sheer immediacy of her. "You never really know what about, eh?" Aziz said, following my eyes. "What...about?" I pressed. "The mathematics of her buttocks moving up and down, in a perfect equation," he replied. *Aesthetics, not mathematics.*

He would attend a mosque in the city from time to time, I must know. "Everyone was so fastidious about how you wash yourself—what the Koran itself does not say...about washing your ears, ankles, and for every part of the body must be clean." *What for?* "It's your soul that must be clean," Aziz concluded.

"The soul?" I asked rhetorically.

He glanced at some young people in the Ottawa park before us smoking hash. "All hooligans," he called them, pronouncing the word *holy-gans.* He remembered about how on one dark night he'd gone on his usual walkabout in the park, and he'd felt absolutely alone, Then he saw a tall woman in a white shroud coming towards him, like an apparition. He was scared.

Really...in Canada.

"This woman told me a bat was chasing after her; I must help her. 'Where's the bat?' I asked her," Aziz said. "It's in the air," the tall slinky woman replied. She looked almost like his first wife, Tabitha...transmogrified. "Can I walk with you now?" the strange woman begged him. "Why?" he drilled. "A bat's coming after me."

"Really a bat?"

Aziz was afraid to walk in the park alone. And would I come with him on his next night's walkabout? *A promise I must make.* And his prevailing dream...to spend one night with a South American beauty he'd first set eyes on in a Soho nightclub when he was a student in London, whom he never forgot.

"South American?"

"It's where you come from, isn't it?" he shot back.

Tabitha: in a white shroud, in another walkabout, he conjured. "I want to go to heaven to be with you," Aziz silently murmured to *her*, closing his eyes. And Rabindranath Tagore's words came back, about being "a wayfarer on an endless road," then "growing like a summer flower magnificently, and dying like an autumn leaf, quietly and beautifully." Words I slowly repeated to myself, and believed.

ACKNOWLEDGEMENTS

Gratitude to Howard Aster of Mosaic Press for his encouragement over many years. Grateful acknowledgement is made to the editors of the following in which some of these stories first appeared: "Welcoming Mr Anang," *The Arts Journal* (Guyana/The Caribbean); "Christine, Interrupted," *An Encounter in the Global Village: Selected Stories*, ed. Hengshan Jin (Shanghai: East China Normal University/dual translation/Chinese-English); "West Meets East," *Short Story Journal* (University of Texas, USA); "My Teaching Days," *The Nashwaak Review* (St. Thomas University, New Brunswick); "The Guitar," *Canadian Fiction Magazine* and *A Second Coming: Canadian Migration Fiction*, ed. D. Mulcahy (Guernica Editions, Ontario); "The House," *South Asia Review* (USA); "Muskeg," *Carousel* (University of Guelph) and in *Canada anglofona: Limba si identitate/*Anglophone Canada: Language and Identity, ed. R. Albu (University of Iasi, Romania); "Making It," *Paragraph* (Toronto); "Forgotten Exiles, *Crossborder* (Leapfrog Press, USA); "The Other Half," *Post-Colonial Text* (UK);

"Jagnath and Tomby," *The Caribbean Writer* (University of the Virgin Islands, USA); "Leovski's Blues," *Kunapipi* (University of Wollongong, Australia) and *Journal of Caribbean Literatures* (Central Arkansas University, USA); "The Well," *Fiction International* (University of San Diego, USA); and "A Father's Son," *Grain* (University of Saskatchewan, Canada). I also thank the City of Ottawa and the Ontario Arts Council for their support.

ABOUT THE AUTHOR

Photo by Frank Scheme

Cyril Dabydeen grew up in Guyana with his earliest years in Canada spent in the Lake Superior region. He attended Lakehead and Queen's universities. His writing is aligned with work in social service and as an educator. He taught writing for many years at the University of Ottawa, and has read his stories in Europe, USA, Canada, the Caribbean, and Asia. Nominated for the IMPAC Dublin Prize for fiction, he won the Okanagan Fiction Prize, the Canute A. Brodhurst Prize, is a prize-winner of the International Conference of the Story in English contest, and a shortlisted finalist of the Ottawa Book Prize (fiction). He has been recommended for a Pushcart Prize via *Prairie Schooner*. His work has appeared in numerous magazines, e.g. *Poetry*/Chicago, *The Critical Quarterly*, *The Warwick Review*, *The Fiddlehead*, *The Queen's Quarterly*, *The Dalhousie Review*, *Prism International*, and in Oxford, Penguin and Heinemann anthologies. He adjudicated for Canada's Governor General's Literary Award and the Neustadt International Prize for Literature (USA). He is Ottawa Poet Laureate Emeritus.